LEAVING
SUTTER'S
BEND

Also by Deanna Madden

Helena Landless

Gaslight and Fog

The Haunted Garden (a novella)

The Wall

Forbidden Places

The World Beyond: A Novel of Ancient Greece

The Box

Storm Country

LEAVING SUTTER'S BEND

DEANNA MADDEN

FLYING DUTCHMAN PRESS

ISBN 978-0-5788-3715-4

Cover design by SelfPubBookCovers.com/RLSather

Flying Dutchman Press

2021

for Doug and Gypsy

Tell me, what is it you plan to do
With your one wild and precious life?
　　　　　　—Mary Oliver, *The Summer Day*

CHAPTER 1

Alec

I've known Jenny my whole life, but not until the party a week after graduation do I really notice her. I'm there with April Evans, who invited me so she wouldn't have to show up without a date, but then soon after we arrive, she decides she'd rather make a play for Tristan Barnett, a linebacker on the football team, and ditches me. Bored and not really in the mood to get high or drunk, I wander out on the porch, thinking maybe I should just go home. Jenny is sitting on the porch steps, staring at the houses across the street as if she can see through them to the wooded hills beyond.

"Why aren't you inside?" I ask, dropping down beside her.

"Why aren't you?" she counters.

"I'm not much of a party person."

"Same here."

Her gaze never wavers from the houses. I look at them but see nothing out of the ordinary. Just your average two-story wood-frame houses with lighted windows silhouetted against the hills under a darkening sky.

"Where are you going in the fall?" I ask her. It's what we're all asking each other. Not everyone is headed off to college, but a lot of us are. I assume Jenny is since she was valedictorian, so I'm surprised when she says, "Not sure I'm going."

"Really, why not?"

She narrows her eyes and keeps staring across the street. In the dead silence that follows, I wonder if I've said the wrong thing. Of course, it isn't really dead silence, not with all that racket from the party behind us. I don't know what's louder, the pounding music or the combined voices of a houseful of grads celebrating. Amazing the neighbors haven't called the cops yet, but the night is young.

"How about you?" she asks.

"Yeah, University of Oregon maybe."

"Why maybe?"

I shrug. "That's where my parents want me to go."

Her eyes flick to me, her attention diverted for a moment. "But not where you want to go?"

"It's a great school," I say noncommittally.

"So why are you less than excited?"

"Not sure I want to go."

She gives me a sidelong glance. "Why not? Don't tell me you want to hang around Sutter's Bend?"

"Sutter's Bend isn't so bad."

"Don't you want to know what else is out there?"

"Probably not much different than here."

"You'd turn your back on the opportunity to get a college education?"

"No," I say, although that's exactly what I've been contemplating. The question is, do I have the courage to tell my parents? A little matter I've been putting off. It's still early in the summer. I have plenty of time before fall to break it to them.

She sighs. "I'd trade places in a heartbeat."

That makes me feel guilty. I shift uncomfortably. "So why aren't you going?"

A small shrug. "Not all of us have rich parents." She resumes staring at the houses across the street as if the answers to the questions of the universe are out there and if she just looks hard enough, she'll find them.

"My parents aren't rich," I object.

She rolls her eyes.

I decide not to argue the point. Maybe from her perspective they are. Her parents own a Chinese restaurant on 7th Street, the Golden Duck. It's something of a hole-in-the-wall place. My dad sells medical equipment for a company in Portland and my mom's a realtor. We live in Bedford Heights, one of the nicer areas in Sutter's Bend.

"Can't you get a scholarship or something?" I ask her.

She's really smart and I figure there must be scholarships for students like her. How could you be valedictorian and not be offered scholarships?

"A scholarship won't cover everything."

Maybe not. I don't know what to say, so I change the subject. "Are you here with Glen?"

"Are you here with April?"

"Yeah, sort of."

I'm surprised she knows about April. We aren't really an item. I'm more a means to an end for April, who, as I said, has her eye on Tristan Barnett. I have no illusion about being competition for Tristan. It was a dumb decision to let her talk me into coming with her, like when Tyler dared me to drink a fifth of Tequila our junior year and I did. When will I learn?

"Shouldn't you go back inside and check on her?" Jenny asks, a not-so-subtle hint which I decide to ignore.

"I doubt she's noticed I'm gone."

We sit there a minute or two in silence while a cloud drifts across the moon. We're not far from the ocean. The air feels cool and damp, as if it may soon rain.

"So if you do go to University of Oregon, what are you going to major in?" she asks, staring at the houses again.

"Premed, I guess."

"You guess?"

"It's what my parents want. Especially my mom."

"So what do you want?"

I shift uncomfortably again. "I don't know. I just know I'm not cut out to be a doctor. I didn't even like dissecting frogs in biology. In fact, I hated it."

The corner of her lip curls as she tries to suppress a smile. "Have you told your mother?"

"Yeah. Not that it makes much difference. She says later I'll be glad I went into premed."

"Maybe she's right."

"I doubt it. She's not the one who had to dissect frogs."

Behind us the screen door flies open with a bang and Marcy Harkness leans out. She has streaks of burgundy in her hair that weren't there last week.

"You guys seen Logan?"

We say no and, disappointed, she ducks back inside.

"I'd give anything to be headed off to college in the fall." Jenny hugs her knees. "I thought I would be, but now my mom says they can't afford it—not me and Paul at the same time."

Paul is her older brother. He was a senior when we were sophomores. Now he's at University of Oregon.

"I'm sorry. That sucks."

"He's studying premed."

Of course, he is. Maybe our parents aren't so different after all.

"What would you major in if you went?" I ask her.

"It doesn't matter. It's not important."

"I'm curious. Come on. I told you mine."

"Okay then. Science. Chemistry. Or maybe physics. I haven't quite decided."

"Physics?" This surprises me, although I'm not sure why. Jenny is brainy. She could be anything she wants.

"Since I was ten years old, I've wanted to be like Marie Curie, you know? I want to make a discovery that's important. Something that will make a difference." Her face looks fierce. Maybe it isn't empty space she sees beyond the houses across the street. Maybe it's the future.

"She died from it," I remind her. "Or did you miss that part?"

"Better that than dying of boredom while I wait tables and cook chow mein."

Jenny works at her parents' restaurant. I feel sorry for her. I wouldn't want to face a future of waiting tables and cooking chow mein either. With a mind like hers it seems an awful waste.

I try to think of something to say that will cheer her up.

"Hey, do you want to get out of here?" I ask.

She glances back at the door, probably thinking about Glen. I wonder how serious they are. Evidently not serious enough for him to be sitting out here on the step beside her. My conscience doesn't bother me about April. She'll find a ride with someone else if she doesn't score a ride with Tristan. And anyway, I doubt she'd think twice about bailing on me.

"Sure. Why not?" Jenny says, getting to her feet.

Even after we're in my car—a secondhand red Camaro with a small dent I got backing into a guard rail—she doesn't ask me where we're going. I get the impression she doesn't care. She's ready to burn bridges and break speed limits. It's just as well she's with me and not someone else.

She doesn't say much as I drive and that makes me nervous. When I suggested leaving, I had in mind driving to a place nearby on the coast where I go sometimes when I'm feeling down or just want to be alone. Now I regret my impulse to take her there. Maybe she won't like it. It's hard to get to, and there's not much there except a little strip of sand and some rocks. I still have time to change my mind and drive somewhere else, but I can't think of where. Sutter's Bend doesn't offer a lot of choices.

When I pull off the road and stop, she still doesn't ask, and I begin to wonder if she's feeling even more reckless than I thought. For all she knows I could be an ax murderer. Of course, I'm not. But just saying. We've known each other since kindergarten. She's as safe with me as if she were my sister. She knows I wouldn't dare make a move on her. All of Sutter's Bend would be ready to lynch me.

Before I have time to climb out, she flings herself out of the car. By the time I join her, she stands on the edge of the drop-off, staring out at the ocean just as intently as she stared at those houses across the street when we were sitting on the steps. It makes me even more uneasy to see her standing on the edge of the drop-off like that. I have to resist the urge to reach out and pull her back a step.

"There's a trail just over here," I tell her and lead the way to the path that drops down to the shoreline. I know where it is since I've been here so many times, but it's not obvious at first glance to someone unfamiliar with it, especially at night.

She does pause when she sees the path, which is narrow and almost a sheer drop to the boulders and sand below, but then she gamely follows as I start down. Descending it in the dark is trickier than going down in broad daylight. Even in daylight you have to be careful of your footing if you don't want to break your neck. In the dark it's even riskier. I hold out my hand and she takes it. It's a bit awkward going down hand in hand, but I know the way and she doesn't. When we reach the bottom, we look out past the boulders at the water, black and choppy under a pale moon.

"What is this place?" she asks.

"I don't think it has a name."

"How come I didn't know about it?"

"Not many people come down here. You can't see it from the water because of the boulders, and there's not much here to come down for. Not big enough for a keg party." I grin.

"Do you come here often?"

"Sometimes."

"Have you brought girls here before?"

I don't want her to think I make a habit of inviting girls down here to make out. I glance sideways at her. "No." Maybe it wasn't such a good idea to bring her here. Why didn't I just take her to the Shack for a Coke?

"I like it," she says, hugging herself.

I feel my shoulders start to relax. Okay, so maybe it wasn't such a stupid idea after all.

The air is chilly. I just hope it doesn't start raining. Climbing back up to the road will be harder in the rain. I should have thought of that before we came down.

"You cold?"

She's wearing a lightweight jacket that looks as if it doesn't provide much warmth.

"A little."

Since she's shivering, I put my arm around her. That's when she looks up at me, and I kiss her. If I'd stopped to think about it, I probably wouldn't have. This isn't some girl I have a crush on. This is Jenny, who I've known practically all my life. She tastes of peppermint and her lips are as soft as a rose petal. I feel something inside me shift. I don't want the kiss to end, and she seems to feel the same. Her eyes are closed, and so I close mine too. Whoever would have thought that Jenny could kiss like this? I force myself to stop before we get too carried away. My breath is a little ragged. Hers is too.

For a moment neither of us says anything. I can hear the waves crashing against the shore.

"So, I'm the first girl you've kissed down here?" she asks, looking around again.

"Yeah." I wonder if I should apologize about the kiss. Is it going to make things between us weird?

She looks at the boulders on the shore, the small strip of sand, and the water slithering up almost to our shoes. Just then the first raindrops start to fall. We scramble to make our way back up the path to my car before a downpour begins.

When I get home later, my nine-year-old brother Toby is watching TV in the living room. I flop down on the sofa for a minute to watch. He sprawls on the carpet a few feet from the screen, propped on his elbows. Mom is always after him about that. She says he'll ruin his eyes. He's watching *Ghostbusters*, although he's seen it a million times already. The Stay Puft Marshmallow Man lumbering through the streets of New York is his favorite part.

I'm hardly settled on the sofa when my mom swoops down the stairs. How she heard me open the door from upstairs I don't know, but that's my mom. Super-sonic hearing. No matter how quietly I sneak in, she always knows when I come home. She's wearing her pink housecoat, her hair wrapped turban-style in a towel, so she probably just showered. Even with her hair wrapped in a towel, you can tell she's a woman who takes pains with her appearance.

"I thought I heard you come in," she says. "Is the party over already?"

"I left early."

"Toby, what did I tell you about lying on the floor while you watch TV?"

My brother doesn't move. He knows she'll give up if he ignores her long enough.

I decide I don't really care about watching *Ghostbusters* for the umpteenth time and haul myself to my feet. Time to retreat to my room before she starts asking questions.

"Did you have fun?"

Here it comes.

"Yeah."

"Were Dustin and Tyler there?"

"No. Tyler has to get up early for work. Dustin wasn't interested. Parties aren't his thing."

"Everything okay?"

"Why wouldn't it be?" I don't know why her question irritates me. Maybe because I just want to be left alone to think about what happened with Jenny tonight, not grilled about how my evening went.

"Well, I didn't think you'd be home so early."

"I got bored." I don't tell her about Jenny. She doesn't know about April either. Of the two she'd approve of April more because her father is on the town council. April is, as my mom would say, *from a good family*. I'm pretty sure she wouldn't approve of Jenny, whose parents live in the south part of town and operate the Golden Duck.

I pass her on my way to the stairs, not sticking around to hear if she succeeds in getting Toby to put more space between him and the TV. Even if she does, it will only be a temporary victory. I'm sure she knows that.

Once up in my room, I put in my earbuds, start my playlist, and grab the paperback I've been reading—a novel about a group of teens getting killed off one by one at a summer camp for delinquents—but after a few minutes of trying to get back into the plot, all I can think about is Jenny. I probably shouldn't have kissed her. Hopefully she understands that I didn't mean anything by it. I feel bad that she isn't going off to college, but there isn't anything I can do about it. It's a shame we can't trade parents. If she had mine, they could send her to college, and if I had hers, I could stay in Sutter's Bend and not worry about being forced to become something I don't want to be.

CHAPTER 2

Jenny

I don't think anyone in my family saw Alec drop me off, which is a relief. Otherwise, I'd have to explain how I happened to be with him and not Glen, and I'd prefer not to have to explain that.

My sister Becca, two years younger than me, is curled up on the sofa with a large bowl of popcorn watching TV when I come in and barely glances up.

"Are Mom and Dad still at the Duck?" I ask.

"Yeah. They let me leave early. Business was slow."

I retreat to my room—actually *our* room since half of it is Becca's—grateful to have it to myself for the moment. I want time alone to think about what happened tonight. Alec Morrissey kissed me. And I let him. In fact, I kissed him back. But now I'm wondering if he kissed me because he felt sorry for me, the valedictorian who doesn't get to go to college because her parents can't afford it. Of course, he didn't *mean* to kiss me. It was an accident, like when you turn too fast with an armful of books and run smack into someone you didn't know was standing there, and your books scatter all over. You're both embarrassed, or at least one of you is, and the other goes blithely on his way. *Sorry. Didn't see you there. No harm done.*

So far as I know, in all the years we've known each other, Alec has never once looked at me, or if he has, it was more as a fellow classmate to compete with and share notes with, not a girl he was inclined to kiss. Afterward, on the ride home, neither of us said anything about the kiss. I was waiting for him to say something, and maybe he was waiting for me to say something. I thought he'd say he hadn't meant to kiss me, but nothing. Just silence. And I wasn't about to bring it up. What could I have said? *Hey, did you mean it when you kissed me?* And if he said no, what then? That would have been even worse than to be left wondering. At least for a while he took my mind off not being able to go to college in the fall. During the drive home, I barely spared a thought to how my parents have dashed my dreams. Who would have guessed that a kiss could make me forget that when it's all I've been able to think about since graduation?

I rummage in my bag for my phone, wondering if Alec will text me, but of course he doesn't have my number. Instead I find a text from Glen. Oh my god. I totally forgot about Glen.

Are you ok? he texted. *What happened to you?*

I should have said something to him before I left the party. I was just feeling so depressed that when Alec suggested leaving, I forgot about Glen. How could I have been so thoughtless?

Got a ride home with Alec, I text back, hoping that will suffice.

I stare at my phone and then lay it aside, hoping it doesn't ring. I really shouldn't feel so guilty. It's not like we're engaged, although we do hang out a lot together. My parents treat Glen as if he's one of the family, like hiring him to help out this summer at the Duck. He's practically like a brother, but I'm not sure that's how he sees it. Anyway, I don't intend to tell him about what happened tonight. It's not really any of his business if I let Alec kiss me.

By morning I figure Alec has forgotten about the kiss, and I tell myself I should too. When I find myself thinking about him, I try to push him out of my mind. But the scene from the night before keeps replaying in my head like a song I can't forget. Even when I go out for a run after breakfast, I find it going through my head.

I almost didn't go to the party last night. It was Glen who talked me into it. He said it would do me good and help take my mind off the University of Oregon. He knows I'm upset about not being able to go in the fall. It's only been a week since my parents broke it to me that they can't afford to send me, and I'm still struggling to come to terms with it. Everyone knows I'm upset, but I'm not supposed to show it. In my family it's frowned on to get angry or complain about anything. That's been drilled into me since I was a kid, a legacy of my Chinese heritage. I'm supposed to just accept it when things don't go my way.

Usually I can hold my feelings in, but this time is different. When Glen and I got to the party last night, I knew right away it was a mistake to come. I couldn't just smile and laugh and pretend nothing was wrong when I felt so miserable. The music was deafening and everyone around me seemed insanely happy, bursting into laughter about things that weren't all that funny, trying to get high or drunk or hook up, or all three. I knew I was a drag on Glen, so I told him I was going outside to get some air, but he should stay and enjoy the party.

I was sitting there on the porch feeling steadily more sorry for myself when Alec wandered out. I thought if I ignored him he would go back inside. But no, he had to plop down beside me and talk about the one thing in the world I didn't want to talk about—going to college in the fall. The next thing I knew I had blurted out like a grade school kid that I wanted to be *a scientist*. I might as well have confessed to wanting to be Queen of England. I have just about as much chance of that happening.

And yet until a week ago I thought I was on track to make my dream a reality. My parents weren't exactly enthusiastic about the science major, but they have always encouraged me to go to college, and I'd been offered a scholarship by the University of Oregon. They thought I should major in premed, like my brother, but I didn't intend to let that stop me from changing my major once I got there. And so when Alec asked what I would have majored in, it just slipped out. So much for self-restraint and suffering silently. My ancestors are probably shaking their heads in disapproval. I'm no doubt a huge disappointment to them. But the injustice of not getting to pursue my longtime dream has been just too much to bear. Almost everyone I know is going off to college. Even Alec is going—or could if he wanted. It shocked me that he doesn't seem to care whether he goes or not. His parents are willing to foot the bill, and yet he's thinking of turning his back on a college education? How can he do that? Doesn't he understand that his future is at stake? So he doesn't want to be a doctor. There must be *something* he wants to be. Doesn't everybody have something they want to be?

By the time I finish my run, I've decided to try to talk Alec into taking advantage of his opportunity to go to college. Maybe I don't have a shot at my dream, but he has a shot at his. It would be incredibly stupid for him to pass it up. And Alec isn't stupid. He raked in A's in Advanced Placement courses. The more I think about it, the more determined I am to talk to him. It's not about the kiss, I tell myself. It's about doing the right thing. Someone needs to tell him not to pass up his chance to go to college. Although the kiss kind of complicates the situation because he might think that's why I want to talk to him. And then there's the problem of *how* to talk to him. I can't very well go over to his house because that would look strange, and now that school is out, it's not like I can stop him in the hall or talk to him in the cafeteria. Then it hits me where I can find him. Foley's Hardware. He's working there this summer. I know because I saw him there a couple of days ago when I went with my dad to buy a new bolt for the backdoor of the Golden Duck. My mind made up, I take a quick shower, grab my bike, and head downtown.

I don't see Alec when I walk into the hardware store, but as I cruise the aisles, I spot his friend Dustin restocking one of the bins in the aisle where the nuts and bolts are sold. I forgot he works here too.

"Hey, Jenny," Dustin calls out before I can retreat. "You looking for something?" His eyes roam the aisle as if he expects to see my father nearby.

"Actually, for someone," I say, deciding maybe he can help by pointing me in the right direction. "Alec Morrissey."

His look of surprise mingled with curiosity makes me instantly regret asking him about Alec. But too late now to retract my words. I do my best to try to look casual about it.

"He's in the lumber section." Dustin jerks his thumb toward the back of the store as a goofy grin spreads across his face.

I thank him and set off in that direction. I probably shouldn't have come. But now that Dustin has seen me, I can't very well leave without trying to find Alec since Dustin is sure to tell him I was here. It will be awkward to explain later why I left without talking to him, so I might as well get it over with.

I find Alec in the back of the store in the lumber section helping a heavy-set man wearing a cap. Alec looks surprised when he catches sight of me but can't abandon his customer. I pretend to examine some boards, as if I'm interested in purchasing them. One of the other workers moseys over and asks if I need help. I say no.

By the time Alec finishes helping the man in the cap, I'm almost ready to run for the door. I can't believe I ever thought coming here was a good idea.

"Jenny, what's up?" Like Dustin, he looks around as if expecting to see my father hovering nearby. Honestly, is it really so difficult to think I might be shopping by myself for something in Foley's?

I take a deep breath. "About the other night . . ."

"What about it?" He looks nervous, as if he's worried what I'm going to say.

" . . . what you said about college. You should go. You'd be crazy not to." I can't believe how tongue-tied I suddenly am. I want to turn and run. This was a mistake.

"You came here to tell me that?"

Well, yes. I see now it was a dumb idea. I wish a hole would open up in the floor and swallow me.

Before I can launch into the argument I prepared in my mind on the way over, a bearded man wheeling a dolly loaded with boards comes around the corner. He stops abruptly, his eyes flitting from me to Alec, like he's trying to decide if Alec is helping me or not. Evidently he decides not and zeros in on Alec. "Kid, can you cut these for me?" He waves his hand at the boards stacked on the dolly. "Or are you too busy?" He smirks.

I feel my face grow hot.

Alec gives me a quick look and then turns to the man, because after all he's a paying customer and I'm not. "Of course, sir."

I watch them walk away. Coming here is turning into a disaster. I should leave.

But then Alec comes rushing back. "Look, how about we talk later? Maybe after I get off work?"

"I have to work later," I tell him.

"I could stop by the Golden Duck."

"No, not there." I can just imagine how my parents—not to mention Glen—would react if Alec showed up at the Golden Duck. Better to keep him away from them for now. I'm not ready to tell Glen or my parents about him. "Sorry," I add, realizing he might think I don't want to talk to him.

At the end of the aisle the man with the dolly looks impatient.

"Then how about we meet at that place I showed you by the water?" Alec suggests.

I hesitate, remembering the isolated spot below the shore road. Maybe I should say no to that too, but it would be a place where we could talk. "Okay. When?"

"How about after I get off at four?"

The time isn't good, but I'll think of some excuse to explain to my parents why I need to be late for work.

"All right, I'll meet you there."

He hurries away to help his customer and I start retracing my steps to the front of the store. As I pass the paint aisle, Dustin springs out as if he's been lying in wait for me.

"Did you find him?" he asks.

"Yes."

"That's good."

As I walk away, I have a feeling he already knew that I found Alec. I just wonder how soon everyone else in Sutter's Bend will know too.

That afternoon I'm a little late when I arrive at the spot on the shore road where a barely visible path leads down to the rocks and the water. Alec's red Camaro is parked on the shoulder of the road. I leave my bike behind it where it won't show from the road and hope no one steals it.

At least this time it's daylight when I make my way down the path. It's a nearly vertical drop, like going down the face of a small cliff, feeling for toeholds and hoping no small rocks give way beneath my sneakers.

When I reach the sand, I see Alec sitting on one of the boulders facing the ocean. I figure he won't hear me over the crash of the waves hitting the rocks, but he turns and waves as I draw near, so he must have been watching for me.

"How'd you get up there?" I shout.

"Climbed."

I tell myself if he managed it, I can too. The boulder is slippery with spray from the breaking waves, but after a bit of effort I manage to join him on it.

"Do you ever climb that one?" I ask, pointing to the next, even larger, boulder.

He shakes his head. "Too dangerous. There are rocks below in the water. Between the rocks and the force of the waves, if you lose your footing and fall, it could kill you."

"Ever tried it?" I ask.

He smiles sheepishly. "Of course."

"I figured."

We sit for a minute and look out at the water, our arms touching. A brisk breeze blows my hair in my face and I push it back again.

"So what did you want to talk about?" he asks, looking sideways at me.

"College."

"What about it?"

"You really should go. Especially since your parents are willing to send you."

He looks at me again. He has brown thoughtful eyes. "Why do you care?"

"Because I can't bear to see you just throw away the opportunity to go to college. Think of all the people who'd like to go and can't."

"Like you?"

"Yes, like me."

"I couldn't believe it when you showed up at Foley's today."

"I'm sorry if I . . ."

"Don't be sorry. I'm glad you came."

"You are?"

"Sure. It's not every day a girl shows up at Foley's looking for me."

I roll my eyes. "I just couldn't bear to know you'd given up something that I would give anything for. I thought maybe I could make you see that it would be a mistake not to go."

"Actually, my parents don't know I'm not going."

"When are you going to tell them?"

He shrugs. "Eventually."

We both look out at the water stretching away to the horizon. Sea and sky seem to merge in a blue haze. I see why he likes it here. We might be miles from Sutter's Bend. Sandpipers peck at the wet sand and gulls swoop and dive.

"Are you sure your parents can't pay for it?" he asks.

"They said we don't have the money. I don't know why it's suddenly a problem. They didn't tell me until the day after graduation. And when I asked why, they wouldn't give me an answer. They just said they were sorry."

"Maybe I could talk to them."

I shake my head. "It wouldn't make any difference."

Not only would it not make any difference, but my parents would be embarrassed if they knew I'd told someone that they can't afford to send me to college. And they would want to know why I'd told Alec. But I'd prefer to keep him a secret for now. Maybe whatever spark we've ignited will quickly burn itself out and they'll never have to know.

He takes my hand. We both look down at his hand holding mine. So am I here because I want to persuade him to go to college or because of the kiss we shared? Before I can make up my mind, our lips meet tentatively again. His arm slides around me. I hear the cry of a gull and the crash of waves breaking on the rocks. For a moment the world seems to hold its breath.

Neither of us says anything when we stop. He keeps his arm around me like it belongs there. I wonder if he can hear my heart beating. I think I can.

"Dustin saw you at Foley's today," he says.

"I know."

"I told him not to tell anyone."

"Thanks."

His thumb explores my palm.

I want to talk about what I'm feeling, but at the same time I'm afraid to for fear of losing it. Whatever is happening between us is too new and precious to analyze. Everything I planned to say slips away. I just want to sit here with his arm around me, feeling him close.

"We should take a picture," he announces, pulling out his phone.

"Yes."

We lean our heads together and smile as he snaps a photo.

"I'll send it to you."

"Thanks."

Then I remember the time.

"I can't stay. I have to go to work. They're expecting me."

Letting go of his hand, I scramble to my feet and spring down from the boulder. When I land on the ground and look back up, he grins.

"Aren't you coming down?" I ask.

"No, I think I'll stay up here a little longer. I like to watch the sun go down."

I glance at the horizon. It will be a while yet before the sun sets. I wish I could stay and watch with him, but I have to go. They're expecting me at the Duck. There will be all sorts of questions if I'm late.

"Jenny," he calls as I turn to leave.

"What?" I look back up at him sitting on the boulder like he belongs there.

"It'll be okay."

The dinner crowd is starting to arrive when I slip in through the back door of the Duck. I grab my apron and duck into the restroom to pin up my hair. Years of practice make this effortless. I hope no one can tell by looking at me that I've just come from being with Alec. I catch a glimpse of myself in the mirror over the sink. Are my cheeks flushed? Hopefully no one will notice.

"Where have you been?" My father is sautéing chicken and mushrooms when I exit the restroom.

"I lost track of time." It's at least partly true.

He frowns. "Next time be more careful. We need here. You know that."

"Where's Mom?" I ask, glancing around.

Glen is preparing an order of shrimp while Becca waits tables in the dining room. As usual, everyone seems to be in motion.

"She didn't feel good," my dad says. "Maybe she'll be in later."

It isn't like Mom to stay home. I wonder if her ulcer is flaring up again. I wish she would see a doctor. She takes Chinese herbs recommended by an acupuncturist one of her friends sent her to, but they don't seem to be helping.

"Here, take this tray to table four," my father says, handing me a tray laden with platters of orange chicken, prawns, and fried vegetables.

Table four is occupied by two couples and a toddler in a highchair. I breathe in the mouthwatering aroma of the food as I set the platters on the table.

"It's about time," snaps one of the women, shooting me a look of annoyance. She has penciled-on eyebrows and red lips that make her look like a kewpie doll. I've waited on her before and she's always rude.

"So sorry for the delay," I murmur, resisting the urge to dump the platter in her lap.

Will I be serving food to rude customers at the Golden Duck for the rest of my life? I think I'd slit my throat. Then I remember Alec sitting next to me on the boulder, his lips on mine and his arm around me. My face feels warm. Thank goodness no one can read my mind.

"Hey, Jenny," Glen says when I return to the kitchen. "What happened to you last night?"

I glance at my father, hoping he's too far away or too preoccupied to hear, but just in case he's not, I lower my voice.

"Didn't you get my text? I got a ride home with Alec Morrissey. I had a headache."

Another half-truth, but this isn't the time or the place to tell him about Alec.

"If you'd told me, I'd have driven you home."

"There was no reason for us both to miss the party."

"How about we go to the Shack after work?"

Ordinarily I'd agree, but what if we run into Alec at the Shack? It could be awkward. "Sorry, I'm tired," I tell him. "I think I'll go straight home afterward."

"You sure?"

"Yes, I'm sure." Now I feel guilty. I know I owe Glen an explanation, but I'm not ready to give it to him—especially not when my father might overhear.

After we close for the night, Becca and I climb into Dad's car. She sits in back, and I sit in front with Dad. As soon as I'm in, I can tell he has something on his mind, but he doesn't say anything right away. We're stopped at a light at an intersection when he says, "Your mother and I understand that you're disappointed about not going to University of Oregon in the fall, but it's not fair to take it out on Glen."

"I'm not taking anything out on Glen. Did he say that?"

"He didn't have to say it. I have eyes. I can see."

All right. Let him think I turned down Glen's invitation to go to the Shack after work because I'm upset about not getting to go to University of Oregon. It's better than trying to explain about Alec.

"You take too much for granted," he says.

I glance at Becca in the back seat. Her eyes are closed and she has her earbuds in and is nodding her head to music I can't hear. I don't blame her for tuning out. I'd do the same if I could.

"What do I take for granted?" I ask since he's probably going to tell me anyway.

"Your family."

Considering that I have to give up my dream of going to college and spend my time for the foreseeable future working at the Golden Duck for less than minimum wage *because* of my family, I think that's an unfair criticism.

"Family is everything," he says solemnly.

I've heard this nugget of wisdom since I was a baby, along with reminders not to talk back, not to be disrespectful, and not to shame my parents. I'm tempted to tell him family *isn't* everything, but of course I can't. I wonder if Marie Curie had to worry about the demands of *her* family.

"One day you will understand this," he adds.

I doubt it. I don't think my parents have the right to decide my future. This isn't China. I'll bet even in China things have changed since they were young.

"Maybe it's time for you to think about marriage," my father says.

My eyes pivot to his profile. *Marriage? Is he serious?*

"*No.* I don't want to get married, and even if I did, it wouldn't be to Glen." I add that last bit because my parents have made no secret of their feelings about Glen. Since we were toddlers, our parents have been pairing us up. There was no harm in it when we were younger, but I draw the line at being nudged into marriage just because our parents would like to see it happen.

The light turns green and we are moving again. I watch the darkened storefronts and the gas stations and the streetlights slide past.

"Why not? He's a nice boy. He'd make a good husband."

"I'm not in love with him."

"Your mother was your age when she got married."

Oh, great. He wants me to live a life like my mother's. Working long hours at the Golden Duck. Having babies. Raising children. Until I'm tired and worn out and my children are grown. It's my parents' vision for my future, not mine. Since grade school they have encouraged me to go to college and pressured me to make good grades so I could get a scholarship, which I did. Now suddenly college is no longer an option. I'm supposed to simply accept this and give up my dream of accomplishing something important in the world. Why has everything changed?

CHAPTER 3

Alec

"Y ou went off and left me there." April's voice quivers with outrage. She stands there glaring at me, her arms crossed.

It's Sunday afternoon, and I'm at the Shack with Dustin and Tyler. I glance around, embarrassed. People are staring. I try to scrunch lower in my chair.

"I thought Tristan might take you home," I tell her.

"Why would you think that?"

I can only shrug since I can't very well say in front of Dustin and Tyler and everyone else within earshot that I'm pretty sure she has a crush on him. She'd kill me. So I try to apologize. "I'm sorry. Something came up."

"What?"

I glance at Dustin and Tyler for help, but they just stay silent, not wanting to attract her wrath. What am I supposed to say? I don't want to mention Jenny. There's no reason to drag her into this. And I suspect knowing I went off with another girl would enrage April even more.

"Fortunately Jeff gave me a ride home."

"Great," I say, maybe a little too enthusiastically.

She scowls at Dustin and Tyler, as if they are also somehow to blame, and then satisfied that she's made her point, she turns and stalks back to her table of girlfriends.

"You ditched her at the party?" Dustin says, keeping his voice low.

"I didn't know you were dating her," says Tyler, stealing a glance at the table of girls.

"I'm not. She asked me to go with her to the party so she wouldn't have to go alone. That's all."

"I thought she was dating Steve," says Dustin.

"They broke up."

"How about you and Jenny?"

"Yeah. What about Jenny?" Tyler asks, leaning forward.

So Dustin told him, even though I told him not to tell anyone. They watch me expectantly, grinning.

"I gave her a ride home. Nothing happened."

Not exactly true. But I'm not about to tell them I took her out on the shore road and down by the water, where we kissed. They may be my best friends, but some things you don't share even with your best friends.

The next day I'm still turning over in my mind the scene with Jenny, torn between wanting to see her again and telling myself it wouldn't work out for any number of reasons, when I run into her by accident at the Bookery.

I go there about once a week to look for books I might want to read. It has new and used books crammed on shelves that rise so high sometimes you have to find a ladder to reach them. The aisles are narrow, but that's one of the things I love about the place. It's like a labyrinth I can get lost in. Best of all, they have a section devoted to horror novels, and I'm always on the lookout for a good horror novel.

I've just pulled down a copy of *Zombie Apocalypse* when I look up and see Jenny at the end of the aisle watching me. I feel as if I've been caught looking at porn. My first instinct is to shove the book back in place on the shelf, but that might look even more suspicious, so I stand there with the book in my hand, waiting to see what will happen.

"You're not working," she says, which is sort of obvious.

"My day off."

She looks as if she's trying to make up her mind whether to make a hasty retreat or stay and talk. She takes a few steps in my direction, glancing with curiosity at the books on the shelves. "You like horror?"

I glance down at *Zombie Apocalypse* in my hand. I can't very well deny it. I try to think of something clever to say, but nothing comes to mind. She's just discovered my secret vice. Will that change her opinion of me?

She smiles. "I wouldn't have guessed. You look so normal."

I try to decide if that's good or bad while she continues closing the gap between us. Evidently she isn't totally put off by my depraved taste in books.

That's when I notice she's holding a book too, and I tilt my head, trying to make out the title.

She glances down at the book, winces, and then holds it up so I can see the cover. *Profiles of Women in Science*. I shouldn't be surprised. She did say she wants to be a scientist.

"Do you come here often?" I ask since I've never noticed her in the Bookery before. But maybe I just wasn't paying attention where Jenny was concerned. That has definitely changed.

She shakes her head. "Not often. Science books are expensive. I usually borrow from the library. How about you? Did you find something interesting?" Her eyes stray to my book.

Too late to hide it now. I hold it up for her to see.

She takes it in her hands, eyes widening. "Oh." She looks so pretty standing there, a half smile on her lips, her hair catching the light from the nearby window, dark eyes meeting mine. Why did I never notice before how pretty she is?

"You know, I don't even have your number," I tell her. "I realized it when I went to send that photo to you."

She hands me back the book. "You didn't ask for it."

I pull out my phone and wait. She gives me her number and watches as I add it to my contacts.

"Would you want to go to a movie sometime?" I ask, trying to sound nonchalant.

"I work most nights."

"Some afternoon then?"

She hesitates. "All right. When?"

"Tomorrow?"

For a few awful seconds I think she's going to say no. But then she smiles. "Okay. Text me. Movie. Time. I'll meet you there."

Yes! I feel like running a victory lap or fist-pumping the air.

Not until she walks away does it occur to me that meeting me at the theater means she doesn't want her parents to know. But that's okay. Maybe it's best to keep our budding relationship under the radar as long as we can. Who knows what malevolent forces in the universe might be unleashed if word gets out that we're dating?

But it isn't malevolent forces or a zombie apocalypse that threatens our first date. It's my mother. On this day of all days it turns out she has to help a fellow realtor who has come down with the flu by showing his client a house. And she doesn't tell me this until I'm about to leave for my date with Jenny. Leaning into the doorway of my room in a red pants suit, her hair swept up in a sort of chignon, she informs me I'll have to watch Toby while she's out.

"I can't. I'm going out," I tell her.

"Alec, I don't ask you to do much," she says, "but you have to do this. I don't want to leave him alone. Last time he tried to microwave popcorn and nearly set the house on fire."

It's been about two weeks since the incident with the microwave popcorn. The house smelled of burnt popcorn for days afterward. Toby has been forbidden to microwave popcorn unsupervised for the indefinite future. Still that's no reason to keep me from taking Jenny to a movie.

"Why don't you call Mrs. Johnson?" I suggest.

"She has a doctor's appointment today."

I wonder if a lethal epidemic is underway. What are the odds? Two people we know sidelined for medical reasons—Mom's realtor friend and the elderly widow down the street who sometimes babysits Toby. But I'm not going to let an epidemic stand in my way. I have a date with Jenny Chen and I intend to keep it.

"Honest, Mom. I can't do this."

"And why not?" She gives me her drill sergeant look.

"I have plans."

"So cancel them."

"I can't."

She levels her deadly X-ray gaze at me. Sometimes I think she has the uncanny ability to read my mind.

"It's *important*," I say.

"So is your brother."

"I *promised* . . ." Actually, that's not true. But I've been looking forward to my date with Jenny since I ran into her at the Bookery yesterday. I can't tell her I can't go because I have to babysit my kid brother. It would be humiliating.

Her eyes narrow with suspicion. "Is this about April Evans? Because if it is, I'm sure she'll understand."

Oh really? She must not know April very well. Besides, it's not about April, although maybe I should let her think it is. Simpler that way. And how does she know about April anyway? I swear my mother has mysterious ways to keep tabs on me. If I didn't know better, I'd wonder if she has my phone tapped.

"You are not to leave your brother here alone," she warns me and then leaves while I'm still protesting.

When I go in search of Toby, I find him in the living room sprawled in front of the TV, playing Lego Marvel Superheroes on his Xbox.

"Come on," I tell him. "We're going out."

"Out where?" His eyes stay glued to the screen, his thumbs keep pushing the controller.

"To see a movie."

"What movie?"

"What does it matter? I'll decide when we get there. Now turn that off or I'll pull the plug."

Twenty minutes later I'm standing in front of the theater with Toby looking over the movie posters. Obviously I can't take him to *Fangs* or *The House That Screamed*. We'll have to go to something PG-rated, and there's really only one choice. *Trolls*. I grit my teeth and fish out my wallet. I've just paid for the tickets when Jenny rushes up in dark glasses looking like an undercover spy. I get the feeling she doesn't want anyone to see her going into the theater with me.

But she takes the choice of *Trolls* in stride and flashes Toby a smile. "Hi, Toby."

"I want to sit beside Jenny," he announces as we walk into the theater.

I can't help noticing how fast he picked up on her name. I'll have to bribe him later not to tell Mom about her.

Jenny is a good sport about it all. "He's cute," she confides as we wait for the previews to begin, Toby hunkered down on one side of her and me on the other. Not the word I would have chosen to describe my brother, and having him tag along is definitely not how I envisioned our first date.

CHAPTER 4

Jenny

I feel guilty that I couldn't hang out with Alec and his brother after the movie, but I didn't want anyone to see us together and for it to get back to my parents. Or Glen. I still haven't told him.

Glen and I dated all through high school. We just kind of got pushed together by our parents, who are friends. Whenever there was a school dance, it was assumed we would go together, and I suppose it was easier to accept the arrangement than fight it. Everybody else thought of us as a couple, so I did too. There didn't seem any harm in it. And it was convenient not to have to worry about whether I'd have a date to a school dance. I figured we'd go our separate ways when we went off to college. The idea that we might someday marry never really crossed my mind. Glen was more of a friend than a boyfriend, someone I could depend on. We made out a few times, but he never pressured me to go farther. I really should tell him about Alec before he hears about him from someone else, but so far there hasn't been a good time to tell him. I can't very well bring it up at the Duck with my family around.

Since meeting Alec, it's like I'm leading a double life, one with my family and another with him. I feel like I have to keep him secret if I don't want to give him up. I know only too well how my parents will react when they find out about him. There's no way they will approve. They want me to find a nice Chinese American boyfriend. Glen fits their expectations; Alec doesn't.

I'd like to keep Alec a secret indefinitely, or at least as long as I can. How hard is that? I just have to be careful no one sees us together. Especially not my parents.

The day after our movie date I get a text from Alec asking me to meet him at the Bookery during his lunch break. I hesitate for only a fraction of a second before agreeing. Of course, it's a risk meeting there, but hardly anyone I know hangs out at the Bookery, and the place is laid out like a labyrinth, so the chances of someone seeing us if we're in an out-of-the-way corner seem slim.

When I arrive, Alec is waiting for me in the horror section, just as we arranged. He breaks into a grin when he sees me, and when I get closer, we kiss—a sort of awkward, self-conscious kiss because we're still shy with each other. I glance back at the end of the aisle, nervous that someone might see us, but we're alone.

"I wasn't sure you'd come," he says.

"Why not?"

"I thought you might chicken out."

"I don't chicken out."

He has three paperbacks under his arm.

"What did you find?" I ask, nodding at the paperbacks, curious.

Looking a little embarrassed, he shows me the books he's holding. The first, *The Night Terror*, has a vampire and a screaming girl on the cover.

"Really? Should I worry?"

"Maybe." He kisses my neck.

I laugh and reach for the second book. *The Stalker*. The cover shows the silhouette of a running woman and a hand holding a bloody knife.

"You really need to expand your reading tastes," I tell him.

On the third cover is a large spider beneath the lurid red letters of the title. *Infestation*.

I roll my eyes. But Alec isn't looking at me. He's staring at the end of the aisle as if he's seen a ghost. I think he's just trying to scare me, but I turn my head anyway. I can hardly believe my eyes. Glen stands at the end of the aisle. I take a step back from Alec, but it's too late. Glen has seen us. Before I can say anything, he's gone. Did he see Alec kissing my neck? Maybe. Oh, why didn't I tell him about Alec?

"I'm sorry," Alec says.

"It's all right. It's not your fault." I glance at the end of the aisle again, but Glen doesn't reappear. I know I should go after him and try to explain. "I'll be back in a minute," I tell Alec.

"Sure."

As I dart through the narrow aisles, I curse myself for not having told Glen sooner. I just hope I can catch him before he leaves. An elderly man in the nature books section looks up startled as I dash past.

I catch up with Glen in the front part of the store as he's almost to the door.

"Jenny," he says, pretending he's surprised to see me.

"I can explain," I say a little breathlessly.

"There's nothing to explain." He puts on a brave smile, which makes me feel even worse.

"I meant to tell you."

"Well, now I know why you've been acting so funny."

"What do you mean?"

"Like you don't want to talk to me, and you're too busy to go out with me."

"I'm sorry."

I glance around. There are a few customers browsing among the new books, but no one seems to be paying any attention to us.

"When were you going to tell me?"

"I wanted to tell you."

"Do your parents know?"

"No. And please don't tell them."

He glances at the door. "All right. But they'll find out sooner or later. You can't hide it forever in a town this size."

"I know," I say, relieved that he'll keep my secret. Later is better than sooner.

Then it occurs to me odd that he just happened to show up at the Bookery when I was meeting Alec. "What are you doing here anyway?"

"I saw your bike outside."

I make a mental note to be more careful next time. If Glen noticed my bike, someone else might too.

"It's okay," he says again. "No hard feelings. Anyway, I've got to go."

I watch him walk out the door. He took it better than I expected. Actually, I'm surprised he isn't more upset. I wonder if he's covering up how he feels. I should have told him. I just hope he keeps his word about not telling my parents. I really don't want to break it to them yet.

CHAPTER 5

Alec

I stare at the three paperbacks in my hands. My meeting with Jenny has not turned out as I planned. I'm not even sure she'll come back. Maybe she'll decide that I was a mistake and it's Glen she cares about most. After all, she's known him much longer, and her parents favor him. Why should a girl like Jenny go for a guy who reads horror novels, works at Foley's, and has no ambition to do anything else? Who am I kidding?

Feeling discouraged, I return the books I'm holding to the shelves where I found them. I'm no longer enthused about reading any of them.

I'm about to leave when Jenny returns. She gives me a rueful smile.

"Did you talk to him?" I ask her.

"Yeah."

"So what did he say?"

"Not much."

"I'm sorry if I caused trouble for you."

"It's my parents I'm worried about. They don't know about you."

"You think they'll be upset?"

She glances at the books on the shelf beside us. "My father told me a few days ago that I should marry Glen."

She says it so matter-of-factly that I can't tell what she's thinking.

"What did you say?"

"What do you think? I said no. I mean, it's bad enough that I can't go to University of Oregon in the fall and that all I have to look forward to is working at the Golden Duck. I'm not going to marry Glen."

I exhale in relief. That's good to know. I mean, the part about not marrying Glen. But if she can't go to college, there goes her dream of becoming another Marie Curie.

She sighs. Her gaze shifts to the window. It looks out on a back lot where a couple of cars are parked. "I need to get out of this town."

"Where would you go?"

"Anywhere that isn't here."

"Maybe we could go together." I say it jokingly, but the idea of losing her when we only just noticed each other makes me feel a little desperate.

Her gaze returns to me. She lays her hand on my arm. "You should go to University of Oregon. Don't throw away your future."

"What about you?"

She shakes her head. "It's not like I have a lot of choice."

"What if your parents met me?"

She gives me a sideways glance. Another shake of her head.

"Would they really hate me?"

"Of course they wouldn't hate you."

I'm not sure I believe her. I want to tell her everything will be okay, but will it? How can I help her? I work at a minimum wage job at Foley's, and my parents won't give me a dime unless it's to attend college.

I try to think of something to say that will make her feel better. She's clearly upset that Glen found out about us. It was bad luck that he came along when he did.

"I should go," she says.

"But you just got here."

"I'll text you later."

I don't want her to go. My brain races as I try to think of something that will persuade her to stay. "Wait. You can't go now."

"Why not?"

I pull out my phone and stare at the screen in mock horror. "Oh my god. It's an invasion. We'll only be safe if we stay here."

She makes a grab for my phone, but I hold it out of reach.

"I lost the signal."

She rolls her eyes. "Is it zombies?"

"Worse than zombies."

"Oh really? What could be worse than zombies?"

"Monsters."

Her eyebrows raise. "Monsters in Sutter's Bend?"

"Or aliens."

"Aliens?"

"You can't leave."

She snaps her fingers. "Maybe we can communicate with them. I'll bet they're intelligent aliens. They'd have to be to get here, right?"

I shake my head. "No, not these. They're drones sent here to enslave us and take over our planet."

"You'd think they would choose someplace more important for their invasion than Sutter's Bend. Why not LA or New York or D.C.?"

"No, that's the beauty of their plan. Start in an off-the-grid backwater like Sutter's Bend where no one will even notice they've arrived."

"But *you* noticed," she points out.

"Yeah, I did."

"You're crazy. You know that?"

"Certifiable. You probably shouldn't leave me here alone. Who knows what I might do?"

"You're so weird, Alec Morrissey."

"Can I see you later? Maybe when you get off work?"

"It'll be too late."

"Then tomorrow at the rocks?"

She touches the side of my face. Her hand feels cool and soft. My heart skips a beat. And then we're kissing again. It's like nothing exists but us—our arms around each other, lips locked, the feel of her body pressed against mine. We're both breathless when we stop. We glance down the aisle guiltily as if Glen might be standing there again. Fortunately he's not.

"This is nuts," she says.

"At the rocks? Tomorrow?"

"When?"

"What time do you get up?"

"What time do you go to work?"

There's that shy smile that makes me want to start kissing her again. She puts her hand on my chest to stop me. "I'll text you."

I make one last effort to prolong the moment. "Are you sure you have to leave?"

"Positive."

I would walk her to her bike, but I know she's worried someone will see us together. Better to say goodbye while we're still in the labyrinth. I'm not sure I could resist kissing her if I walk her to her bike.

After she leaves, I browse a little longer, but my heart's not in it. I keep seeing Glen standing at the end of the aisle. Maybe it was just as well he saw us. If everyone knows, we won't have to sneak around and meet in secret. But what if he tells her parents about us? Suppose they turn against me before they ever have the chance to get to know me? Whatever's happening between us could be over before it's barely begun. The more I think about it, the more precarious it all seems. Too much hinges on whether Glen will keep our secret. If I were in his shoes, would I keep us secret? I doubt it. I'd probably blurt out the truth to her parents at the first opportunity I got if I thought it would help me fend off a rival.

That settles it. Jenny has to tell her parents before Glen ruins everything. I look at my phone. My thumb hovers over the screen as I debate whether to text her. The problem is, even if she tells them, it's no guarantee they'll accept me. They don't know me. They've never met me. It's easy to judge someone you've never met. And so maybe it's time for Jenny's parents to meet me.

CHAPTER 6

Jenny

When I walk in the door of the Golden Duck, I look around nervously. Since leaving the Bookery earlier today, I've worried Glen will tell my parents about Alec even though I asked him not to. The more I've thought about it, the more uneasy I feel. He might think he's doing the right thing by telling them, that my parents have a right to know. He might even see it as protecting me. Crap. I should have told him about Alec sooner. I could have broken it to him gently. I don't really think he's mad at me. Glen is one of the mildest people I know. He practically never gets mad at anyone. But I've hurt him. Even mild people have their limits.

And if Glen does tell my parents, it isn't like they're going to disown me. At worst they'll make me feel like they're disappointed in me. I can survive that, can't I? It wouldn't be the first time I've disappointed them.

As I walk into the kitchen, I glance at Glen. He stands a few feet from my father chopping up pieces of chicken and doesn't look up. I slip into the restroom, pin up my hair, and tie on my apron. My father is stir-frying vegetables when I come out. Through the gap above the counter I can see most of the dining room—a scattering of customers sitting beneath red Chinese lanterns, tables spread with white tablecloths, Chinese characters on the pillars, prints of famous Chinese landscape watercolors on the walls. My mother is standing next to the nearest table chatting with a customer. She looks small and elegant in her grey silk dress. Evidently she's feeling better today.

"Jenny." My father points at a tray holding three bowls of egg flower soup. "Table three."

I nod and reach for it. Nothing seems out of the ordinary, so gradually I begin to relax. I can talk to Glen later.

More customers arrive as the evening progresses until nearly all tables are occupied. Becca and I rush from table to kitchen and Glen helps us whenever he can. I've just returned a customer's credit card when Alec walks in. He stands by the door looking lost, and then our eyes meet and he smiles. I hurry across the room to reach him before Becca does.

"What are you doing here?" I keep my voice low, although with all the conversations and general clatter no one is likely to hear me. I can't imagine what could be so urgent that he has come to the Golden Duck to find me.

"I thought maybe I could meet your parents," he says, his eyes darting around the room as if looking for them.

"*Now?*" I glance around the crowded dining room. My mother is still talking to the same customer, an elderly woman with her husband, and hasn't noticed him. I look toward the kitchen. Through the gap over the counter I see my father and Glen. My father is looking down, intent on the order he's preparing. Glen, on the other hand, is watching us.

"This isn't a good time," I say hastily. "Why don't you call me later?" I block his way, hoping he will take the hint and leave.

His attention is riveted on the gap over the counter. He too must have noticed Glen is watching us. "Did he tell them about us?"

"No."

At that moment Glen turns to my father and says something. My father looks directly at us and my stomach drops. I worry Glen has just told him about Alec and me. But before I can get Alec to leave, his attention is caught by something else. A quick look over my shoulder shows me my mother walking toward us. Too late now to hustle him out the door.

"Let me handle this," I tell Alec.

"Jenny, is everything okay?" my mother says behind me.

I turn and face her with a smile. "Everything's fine."

"Are you going to introduce me to your friend?"

I glance at Alec and try desperately to think of a reason to explain why he's here. Before I can, he speaks up.

"I was hoping to talk to you," he tells my mother. "That is, if you don't mind and you have a few minutes?"

No, no, no. This isn't happening.

"We're very busy right now," I tell Alec.

"Jenny, where are your manners?" my mother scolds. "Of course, I have time to talk to your friend."

I watch helplessly as she leads him to a table for two against the wall. Then I hurry after them. Alec sits on one of the chairs and she on the other. Since there are no other chairs, I stand beside them. No way am I going to leave him alone with my mother. I don't know what he's going to say. I just hope he's not going to tell her about the place with the rocks on the shore where we went after the party or how we met earlier today at the Bookery. What he does say takes me by surprise.

"Jenny's really smart." He glances up at me.

Not exactly a beginning that reassures me, and so I worry what he's going to say next. How could he have thought coming here was a good idea? If I had wanted to think of a bad way to introduce him to my mother, I could not have come up with a worse. Except maybe a car accident. One in which his car slammed into ours. Yes, that would definitely have been worse.

"I know this," my mother says and waits for him to continue.

Alec's eyes lift to me again in a mute plea for help and then move back to her. I feel like I'm watching a disaster unfold in slow motion and I'm helpless to stop it.

"Go take care of our customers," my mother tells me with a small wave of her hand, dismissing me, but I don't budge.

"Jenny should go to college," Alec says.

I could groan. Is that what this is about? My mother waits with hands folded for what else he will say. I'm waiting too. I just hope it doesn't include a zombie apocalypse.

"She deserves to go to college," he says. "If anybody in our class deserves to go, it's Jenny."

"I agree," my mother says, "but we don't always get what we want. Jenny understands this."

Do I? We're talking about my future here, not a dress for prom.

I look at Alec, wondering what other arguments he can come up with. But he seems to have run out of them already. Maybe my mother's calm, expectant face is unnerving him.

Just when I think things can't get worse, my father joins us, wiping his hands on his apron. Of course I have to introduce him to Alec. He shakes Alec's hand. How many of the customers are watching us? I'm afraid to look.

"You're a friend of Jenny's?" my father says. "Nothing wrong, I hope?"

"No, I just wanted to say . . ." Alec's eyes meet mine.

Don't. Please don't.

"He says Jenny is very smart," my mother tells my father, as if I'm not standing right there.

"Yes, she is," my father agrees.

"He thinks she should go to college."

"Yes, she should."

It's maddening how agreeable they are. You'd think they were the most agreeable parents in the world.

"Isn't there some way for her to go?" Alec asks, looking from one to the other, as if he still believes he can persuade them. He doesn't understand my parents. They will smile and be polite, and not a word he says will make any difference.

"We can't afford it right now. Jenny knows that." My father casts a reproachful look at me as if Alec's being there is my fault, and I suppose it is. "Was there anything else?"

Alec shakes his head, looking discouraged. I could have told him he's not going to change their minds. Regardless of how agreeable they seem, it's like arguing with a rock wall.

Reluctantly he stands, his chair squeaking on the tile floor as he pushes it back. He says goodbye to my parents and glances apologetically at me. I walk to the door with him, not daring to look back.

"I'm sorry," he says. "I thought if I explained to them—"

"It's okay," I assure him. "Call me later."

I close the door behind him. When I turn, Becca signals frantically for me to help wait tables. And so I do, one eye on the door, wondering if Alec will come back. Customers leave and more arrive. After seating the new arrivals and doling out menus, I look around for my mother. She's still sitting at the table for two, frowning at the white tablecloth as if she has noticed a spot on it but is trying to decide whether to just leave it or do something about it. I walk over to her, knowing I should explain about Alec.

"I'm sorry. I didn't know he was going to come here."

She sighs. "I thought you and Glen . . ." Her voice drifts away, as if it's too much effort to finish her thought. She looks tired. I feel a pang of guilt.

"No." I glance at Glen in the kitchen, his head bent over the order he's preparing. "No, we broke up."

CHAPTER 7

Alec

I feel terrible when I leave the Golden Duck. Going there was a big mistake. I didn't help the situation, and maybe I made it worse. I wouldn't blame Jenny if she never spoke to me again.

I think about her all the way home, and by the time I get there I've decided to ask my dad to use my college fund for Jenny to go to the University of Oregon instead of me. Only problem—he's five hundred miles away in Toronto at a convention for the latest in medical equipment. I'll have to wait until he comes home to ask him.

When I walk into the house, Toby is sprawled on the floor of the living room watching TV. I envy him. He has no clue how stressful life is going to be nine years from now.

"Hey, Toby. When's Dad coming home?"

"Dunno."

"Where's Mom?"

"Kitchen."

Since this is as much as I'll probably get out of him, I leave him to his TV program and head for the kitchen, where I find my mother sitting at the table sipping a glass of red wine and looking at a magazine. The sight pulls me up short. Since when does she drink wine in the evening? Not that she doesn't ever drink. I just don't remember seeing her drink *alone* before. But my dad isn't home, and it's not really any of my business, so I don't say anything about the wine.

"When's Dad coming home?" I ask.

She shrugs. "I have no idea."

Her answer strikes me as strange. He's been gone more than a week. Why doesn't she know when he's coming home?

"Why do you want to know?" she asks as an afterthought.

"I want to ask him something."

"What?"

I know I have a better chance of persuading my dad to give me the money for Jenny than my mom. She'll not only turn me down. She'll want to know why I'm trying to help Jenny, and that will be hard to explain without letting her know I'm seeing Jenny.

"It's not important," I tell her and turn to leave.

"Alec."

"Yeah?"

"I don't know when your father's coming back."

"You already said that."

"The truth is he may not be coming back at all."

"What do you mean?" I glance nervously at the doorway, my nearest avenue of escape. It's only a few steps away. So close and yet so far. Something tells me I don't want to hear what's coming next.

"We're getting divorced."

I feel as if I've just walked into a bad movie, one that I don't want to be in. I look around at our brightly lit kitchen with its cooking island, granite countertop, and dark wood cabinets. Everything in its appointed place.

Just like that she breaks it to me.

I've known kids at school whose parents have gotten divorced. Was this how they found out? One of their parents just casually announced it? I always imagined divorcing parents had a huge fight and then one walked out the door, slamming it behind them and driving off in a squeal of tires. Not like this.

"You don't have to worry," she tells me. "You'll be able to go to University of Oregon in the fall just like we planned."

She makes it sound like divorce is a minor inconvenience. I know better. If my parents divorce, nothing will ever be the same. Toby and I will probably be scarred for life. There will be shouting matches about how things will be divided. Including us.

"He's got a girlfriend," my mother says. "A girlfriend with a *kid*." As if a kid makes it even worse.

"So he's not at a convention in Toronto?"

She looks down at her magazine. "Like I said, you don't have to worry."

I wish she'd stop saying that. How can she turn my world upside down and act like it's no big deal?

"I don't want to study premed." It seems as good a time as any to tell her. Maybe I'm feeling a bit angry.

She frowns. "Of course you're going to study premed. It's been decided."

"Not by me."

"Be reasonable. What happens between your father and me doesn't need to interfere with your college plans."

"I don't want to be a doctor."

"How can you know if you haven't even tried?"

Does she think I have to make my way through medical school and spend a few years setting broken bones and taking out appendixes in order to know I'm not cut out for it?

"In fact, I'm not sure I want to go to college at all." There, I said it. I feel like a weight has been lifted. No more pretending that I'm going to go along with their plans for me.

"Alec!" She stares at me.

You'd think I just announced I was going to rob a bank or shoot somebody. At least I've got her attention now.

"So I suppose you intend to just keep working at Foley's?"

"I don't see what's wrong with that."

"You're just saying this to upset me."

"No, I'm not."

"Honestly, Alec. You think I'm not already upset enough about your father? For once couldn't you think about someone besides yourself? Do you expect your father and me to support you forever?"

"You want me to move out?" I snap back.

We glare at each other.

"No, I want you to go to college like we planned. I want you to make something of yourself, not end up in a dead-end job scraping to get by."

"You mean you want me to be like you and Dad. How's that working out?" It's a low blow, but I can't help myself.

She looks at me as if I slapped her. Tears well up in her eyes. Maybe I did go too far.

"Sorry," I mutter and leave the kitchen before I say anything else I'll regret. I storm upstairs to my room, close the door, and throw myself on my bed. A few minutes later I try to call my dad. His phone rings repeatedly until it goes to voicemail and an automated voice asks me if I want to leave a message. What do I say? I want to know if it's true that he and my mom are going to divorce. Maybe he'll tell me it's all a misunderstanding. Maybe there's no girlfriend with a kid. Time runs out before I can make up my mind what to say and the dial tone cuts me off. Feeling defeated, I jam in my earbuds and try to drown out my thoughts with my playlist.

CHAPTER 8

Jenny

My parents don't say anything about Alec on the way home. I thought there would be a scene but there isn't. In a way this is worse. They sit in the front seat in stony silence. Next to me Becca is plugged into her music again. She knows about Alec now. Like everybody else at the Golden Duck tonight, she saw him talking to my mother. After he left, she asked me about him the first chance she got, grabbing my arm as I cleared the dishes off one of the tables and nearly making me drop a plate.

"Is he your boyfriend?" she demanded.

I denied it, but I could see she didn't believe me.

"Does Glen know?"

We both glanced toward the kitchen, where Glen was busy stir-frying prawns.

"Yes, he knows."

Since my parents don't make a scene in the car, I expect it to come when we get home, but again it doesn't. It's like they've decided to ignore Alec's visit tonight. They'll pretend it didn't happen and everything will go back to the way it was.

But later when Becca and I are getting ready for bed and I'm checking my phone messages to see if there's anything from Alec, my mother comes into our room.

"Becca, can you give us a few minutes to talk?" she asks.

My sister groans and reluctantly leaves. When she's gone, my mother sits down beside me on the bed. There are dark circles under her eyes that I never noticed before and streaks of grey in her hair. When did she start looking so old?

I know she's going to ask me about Alec, so I rush to explain before she says anything.

"I'm sorry about Alec. I didn't know he was going to show up tonight."

"When he said he had something to say, I thought . . ." Her voice trails away. She lifts her hand to her forehead as if she has a headache.

What had she thought—that I might be pregnant? Did that cross her mind? Surely not.

She tries again. "So you and Glen have broken up?"

"Yes."

"How long . . . ?"

"Not long."

"What happened? Did you have a fight?"

"No, it wasn't like that."

"This boy who came to the Golden Duck tonight . . ."

"Alec." I want her to know he has a name.

"How long have you . . . ?"

"Not long."

"Why didn't you tell us about him?"

"Because I knew you wouldn't approve."

I wait for her to deny it, but she doesn't.

"You and Glen have always got along so well together."

"As friends, nothing more."

"What do . . . *Alec's* parents think about this?" She says his name as if trying it out.

"I'm not sure they know."

She sighs. "I just don't want you to get hurt."

"I can take care of myself," I tell her.

She tucks my hair behind my ear. "I know you're upset about not being able to go to college in the fall."

I stiffen. I don't want to discuss it again. I know I have to accept it. That doesn't make it easy. I can put up a front— that's what she wants to see—but chip away at it and I may start saying things I shouldn't, or worse, burst into tears.

She puts her hand on my arm. "Life is short, Jenny. When you're young, it feels like you have forever, but you don't. I just don't want you to . . ." She touches the side of my face, her hand cool and featherlight. "You remind me so much of myself when I was young."

I can't imagine that she was ever like me. If she was, what happened to her? Did some fire inside her get extinguished? Was she forced to give up something she really wanted? Because that's what she's asking of me—to give up my dream of being a scientist and pretend that I'm content with a life I don't want.

"About this boy . . . "

"Alec."

"Someday when you're older you'll understand."

I think I understand right now. She wants me to live a life like she's lived. And I can't. I won't.

My phone rings. I know by the ring-tone that it's Alec. But I can't answer with my mother sitting beside me on the bed. She glances at the phone, sighs, and then stands. Not until the door closes behind her do I grab my phone and answer.

"I'm so sorry," Alec says. "Can you forgive me? It was a dumb idea to go there. I should have listened to you."

"It's okay. You were just trying to help."

"What did your parents say?"

"My mother thinks your parents won't approve of me."

A pause. "They're getting divorced. I just found out."

I can tell he's upset.

"Oh, Alec. I'm sorry."

"I just wasn't expecting it, you know? I'm still trying to get my head around it."

"What about college in the fall?"

"My mom said I can still go."

"That's good."

"I told her I don't want to be a doctor."

"What did she say?"

Another pause. "I also told her I don't want to go to college."

"Alec—"

"So I guess I'll be here when fall comes, same as you. We can hang out together." He says it like it's a good thing.

The door flies open and Becca bursts in. She flings herself down on her side of the bed and looks at me expectantly. I glare at her but it makes no difference. She doesn't care if I'm on the phone with Alec. Privacy in this house is nonexistent.

"I have to go," I tell Alec. "I'll talk to you tomorrow."

"See you at the rocks in the morning?" he asks hopefully.

"I'll try."

Becca is grinning when I get off the phone. "Was that *him*—lover boy?"

"Don't you have anything better to do?"

"Did Mom tell you to break up with him?"

"No. Why should she?"

"I heard Dad tell her in the kitchen that you should break up with him."

My sister can be annoying, but I have the sinking feeling that in this case she's telling the truth. "What did she say?"

"She said she was tired and they could talk about it tomorrow."

So I get a short reprieve. But if Becca's right, they're going to pressure me to break up with Alec. Not that I'm surprised, but it's so unfair. First I have to give up college. Now I have to give up Alec? What kind of life will I have if I have to give up everything I want?

"It's your turn to get the light," Becca reminds me as she lies down and burrows under the covers.

I really don't feel like going to bed yet, but sharing a room requires compromise. No reason to keep Becca awake just because I'm upset. So after I turn off the ceiling light, I snap on the small desk light beside my bed.

"I'm going to read for a bit. I don't feel like sleeping yet."

She groans, but I know she'll be asleep in five minutes. She's used to me reading at night when I can't sleep. I envy her her ability to fall asleep as soon as her head hits the pillow. Meanwhile, I have a choice: lie awake and think about all the things going wrong in my life or read a book. I choose to read a book.

Reaching under the bed, I pull out the most recent book I've stashed there—*Profiles of Women in Science*. I've only read the first chapter so far. Now I flip pages, looking ahead. Each chapter profiles a different woman scientist and includes a photo of her. One photo in particular catches my attention—a striking-looking woman in a white lab coat, her hair pulled back in a bun, staring straight into the camera. Clara Weisberger, a microbiologist who made an important breakthrough in developing a vaccine for the swine flu virus. I'm not sure what it is about her that draws me to her. Maybe her clear-eyed stare or maybe the determined lift of her chin, as if she's not going to let anything stand in her way.

Soon I'm caught up in her story. It seems she always knew she wanted to study science. After her parents died in a car accident, she was raised by her grandparents on a farm in Minnesota. They didn't have much money, but she went to college on a scholarship. When she was twenty, she had an illness that forced her to drop out of college for a while. There were other obstacles after that, but she never gave up on her goal. When I finish reading the profile, I glance at Becca, who's now fast asleep. She looks as if an earthquake wouldn't wake her. I turn back to the book open in my lap and notice a note in small print at the end of Clara Weisberger's profile. I can hardly believe my eyes. She lives right here in Oregon.

CHAPTER 9

Alec

As soon as my mom and Toby leave, I dash upstairs to my parents' bedroom. Last night when I couldn't sleep it occurred to me how I can find out if my dad's really left. I can check his closet and dresser drawers. At first glance the room tells me nothing. The framed photo of my parents on their wedding day still stands on the dresser and so does the one of Toby and me taken at Disneyland when I was fourteen and he was five. I slide open the closet door. A lot of my dad's clothes are still hanging in the closet. That might be a sign he hasn't moved out. But when I pull open his dresser drawers, they're half-empty. Definitely not good. I sit down on the bed and try to call him again. When the call goes to voicemail, I hang up. What's the point of leaving a message? What am I supposed to say?

I try Jenny next but no luck there either. And she's not returning my texts. Not that I can blame her. Showing up at her parents' restaurant like I did was a big misstep.

With nothing better to do, I drive to the rocky shoreline north of town where I took Jenny the night of the party, hoping she'll turn up, but after an hour of waiting, it's still just me and a host of busy little sandpipers pecking about in the sand. Finally I give up and go home to shower and change before heading to work.

I don't really feel like going to work, but I don't want to lose my job at Foley's either. Fortunately, waiting on customers doesn't require much effort. A brain-dead zombie could do this job, which is just as well since I can't get Jenny off my mind. If only I hadn't gone over to the Golden Duck to talk to her parents! I finally find a girl I really like, and I blow it. Way to go, Morrissey.

"What's the matter?" Dustin asks when we're on our mid-morning break in the break room.

"Nothing."

"Right. You always look like someone just ran over your pet gerbil."

"My what?"

"Does this have anything to do with a certain girl?"

"What do you mean?"

He rolls his eyes in mock exasperation.

"Okay, yes. Jenny isn't answering her phone. I did something really stupid last night. I went over to her parents' restaurant."

"So?"

"Her parents didn't know about me."

"Uh-oh."

"I thought I could persuade them to send her to college."

"She's not going to college?" He looks surprised.

"No. And now she's not answering my calls or returning my texts."

"Maybe her phone's not working."

"That's not all. I just found out my parents are getting divorced." I rub my temples. "I don't know what to do."

"That sucks."

"Yeah, tell me about it."

He brightens. "Hey, I got it. Want to go to the Shack after work and grab a burger?"

A burger is Dustin's go-to remedy for all of life's problems. What can't be solved by a burger loaded with half a dozen toppings?

So after work we head for the Shack. By now I'm beginning to seriously consider Dustin's suggestion that Jenny's phone may not be working. After all, last night she said everything was okay. Of course, that was before she had a night to sleep on it. Maybe she woke up this morning and came to her senses, compared me to Glen, and realized the mistake she'd made.

When I get home, I'm still feeling lousy. A faded grey Buick is parked in front of our house. If it's one of my mother's friends, I hope they're in the kitchen so I can slip into the house without being noticed. I don't feel like talking to anybody, especially not my mother's friends. I just want to go to my room and lose myself in a truly scary novel.

I should have known it wasn't the kind of car a friend of my mom's would drive. When I walk in the house, my mom's sitting in the large armchair in the living room across the coffee table from Jenny's father. Meanwhile, Toby's apparently been banished to his room.

"Alec, I believe you know Mr. Chen," my mother says in her best hostess voice.

"Uh, yes." I nod at him, wondering if he has come to complain to my mother about me showing up at the Golden Duck last night. Or to ask me to stay away from Jenny. Maybe both. He's a small man, greying hair and stooped. I shouldn't feel intimidated.

"He's been waiting for you to come home." My mother looks pointedly at me.

Of course, what she's really saying is I'm late and she has had to sit here making small talk with him instead of doing something else she'd rather be doing.

"I stopped by the Shack," I offer by way of explanation.

She ignores my excuse. "It seems his daughter is missing." The way she says it suggests I'm to blame.

"Missing?" How can Jenny be missing?

"He thinks you know something about it." The look she's giving me is the same sort of look she gave me last Halloween when some local teens wrapped a tree in the principal's yard in toilet paper. Why is it she always suspects the worst of me? Whatever happened to being innocent until proven guilty?

"Why would I know something about it?"

"He says you and Jenny"—she glances at Mr. Chen—"are dating." She says it as if I've done something shameful.

"We went on *one* date."

"So it's true."

I hear the disapproval in her voice.

Mr. Chen turns to me. "Please. We just want Jenny to come home."

"Sorry. I don't know where she is." I glare at my mother.

"Are you sure?" she asks, as if she suspects me of not being entirely truthful. What does she think—that I murdered Jenny and hid the body?

"Yes, I'm sure. I've been waiting all day for her to phone." The words are no more than out of my mouth when it occurs to me that if Jenny's missing it may explain why I haven't heard from her.

"This isn't like Jenny," her father says, shaking his head. "To go off and tell no one where she's going."

I force myself to focus on what matters here—Jenny is missing. So where is she? Could she have met with foul play? Been kidnapped or abducted?

"Have you called the police?"

"Yes."

"So are they going to look for her?"

He stares abjectly at the carpet. "No."

"Why not?"

He looks helplessly at my mother and then at me. "She left a note. She said not to worry. She had to go away for a while."

She left a note?

"That's why the police won't search for her.

"And she didn't say where she was going?"

He shakes his head. "I thought you—" His voice breaks.

He thought I would know where she was because I showed up at the Golden Duck last night to plead her cause. But honestly does he think I wouldn't tell him if I knew?

"Well, I guess Alec can't help you," my mother says, abruptly standing.

Mr. Chen takes the hint and also stands. He looks at me, his eyes pleading. "If you see her, can you give her a message please?"

I nod.

"Tell her . . ." He looks around the room as if looking for the words. "Tell her that her mother has cancer."

Cancer? I stare at him, seeing in my mind the frail hollow-eyed woman who sat across the little table from me at the Golden Duck. I should have guessed something was wrong.

"Jenny doesn't know?"

He shakes his head again, tears in his eyes. "No. We haven't told her yet."

Before I can blurt out, *why not?* my mother intervenes. "I'm sorry. Of course Alec will tell her if he sees her."

She keeps up a steady stream of empty reassurances as she walks him to the door. As soon as he's gone, she wheels on me. "Is there anything else you haven't told me?"

"It was *one* date."

"I thought you were dating April Evans."

I refuse to have this conversation with my mother. Who I date is none of her business. And I don't need her permission to date Jenny. This is my life and I'll date whoever I want. I turn on my heel and head for the stairs.

"Where are you going?"

"To my room."

As soon as the door closes behind me, I check my phone again. No message from Jenny or my father. I don't know which disappoints me more. Jenny, I suppose. She left a note for her parents but not for me. That stings. I guess I underestimated her feelings for me. But then I remember how it felt when we kissed. Surely I didn't imagine the electricity between us? No, I refuse to believe I meant nothing to her unless she tells me herself.

So where is she? She didn't just disappear into thin air. Maybe she went to a friend's house. Someone must know where she is. It's not like we're in New York or LA. People don't just disappear in Sutter's Bend.

The next morning I set out to search for Jenny. While her father probably contacted Megan Murphy, her best friend, I have to start somewhere and Megan seems as good a place to start as any. I don't have her phone number, but I know where she lives on Jefferson Street, so I go there and ring the bell. After all, what do I have to lose? Do I really care if all Sutter's Bend knows I'm looking for Jenny Chen? If Jenny minds, I'll apologize to her later after she turns up. Maybe next time she'll leave me a note.

"Alec!" Megan looks surprised when she sees me.

I thought Jenny might have told her about me since they're best friends, but apparently not. Maybe I should just wear a T-shirt with *I heart Jenny* emblazoned on the front.

"I'm looking for Jenny Chen. Any idea where I might find her?"

"Sorry, no. Her father called here yesterday looking for her. What's up?"

"She seems to have disappeared. I thought maybe since you're her best friend . . ."

She shakes her head. "Sorry. I have no idea where she is."

I look beyond her, wondering if she's telling the truth. A large potted plant blocks my view of the room behind her. Could she be hiding Jenny? Suppose Jenny had a fight with her parents and wanted a place to stay while she sorted things out.

Wouldn't her best friend be willing to provide that? Too bad I can't barge in and search for her. "Do you know anyone else who might know?"

She frowns, thinking. "Glen might."

I really don't want to talk to Glen. "I think they broke up."

"Really?" Evidently Jenny didn't tell her this either.

She waits for me to explain, but I don't intend to.

"You have no idea where she might have gone? She never mentioned somewhere she might want to go?"

"Not that I can think of." Then she snaps her fingers. "New York."

New York? Why would Jenny suddenly pick up and go to New York? Maybe there's a lot about Jenny I don't know.

"Why New York? Does she know someone there?"

"I don't think so. It's just a place she mentioned wanting to visit."

I doubt Jenny ran off to New York because it's a place she'd like to visit someday. "Are you sure there's no one else who might know where she is?"

"Have you asked her sister?"

"Her sister?"

"Yeah, Becca."

In a flash I remember the younger girl helping out at the restaurant. Jenny's sister. If she knew where Jenny was, wouldn't she have told her parents? It doesn't seem like a helpful lead, but maybe I should check it out.

Megan regards me with frank curiosity. "So you volunteered to help her parents look for her?" I can almost see the little cogs and wheels turning in her brain as she tries to fit the pieces together. She hasn't quite reached the conclusion

69

that I could be more to Jenny than just a former classmate, but she's moving in that direction.

"How do I get hold of her sister?"

"You could go over to their house."

No, I couldn't. I doubt I'm welcome there. Maybe she sees that on my face.

"Or you might try the Shack. Becca goes there sometimes with her friends."

Grateful for the tip and relieved to be done with the awkward conversation, I thank her and head for the Shack, although what are the odds that Becca will be there at this hour? And I'm not sure I'd recognize her even if she is. Still, I might as well give it a shot.

It's still early when I walk in. The lunch crowd won't descend on the place for a couple of hours yet. I spot some high school girls huddled in one of the booths, but none looks familiar. No sign of Dustin or Tyler. But then Tyler's probably at work. I order a shake and park myself at a small table next to a window while I check my phone again. Still nothing from Jenny or my dad. I send a text to Dustin to let him know I'm at the Shack. He lives only a couple of blocks away, and before I finish my shake, his battered pickup pulls into the parking lot.

"What's up?" he asks, sliding onto the chair across from me a few minutes later.

"Jenny's disappeared."

He looks at me blankly. "What do you mean—disappeared?"

"Just that. No one knows where she is."

"You mean, like alien abduction?" He grins.

"I'm serious."

"Maybe she's ghosting you. Girls do that all the time."

Do they? Since when is he an expert on girls? Aside from taking Nancy Carpenter to the Senior Prom, I don't think he's ever been on a date.

"Her father came to my house."

"No kidding?" His eyes go wide.

"Look, do you know her sister Becca?"

"Yeah. A freshman. Well, sophomore now, I guess. Why?"

"Is she with that group of girls over there?" I nod at the booth of high school girls.

Dustin turns and looks them over. "Nope. So why are you looking for her sister?"

"Megan Murphy said maybe she would know something about Jenny's disappearance."

"Don't you think if Jenny wanted to talk to you she would?"

It's the same question I've been asking myself, but I don't need to hear it from him.

"Suppose she can't?"

"What do you mean?"

"Suppose she's tied up somewhere. Or suppose she's unconscious."

"Like in a coma?" He drums his fingers on the table. "Hang on." He goes up to the counter. When he comes back, he's carrying a plastic tray loaded with a Monster Burger, fries, and a shake.

"If she's really disappeared, why aren't the police looking for her?" he asks as he prepares to bite into his Monster Burger.

"Because she left a note."

"A note?" He raises an eyebrow.

"She left a note for her parents, but she didn't say where she was going or why."

"Well, there you go. You just have to wait for her to come back."

Maybe he's right, but I feel like it's my fault Jenny has run off in the first place. I can't help feeling her disappearance is connected to my visit to the Golden Duck. And if her mother has cancer, she needs to know that. I have to find her. If she tells me she doesn't ever want to speak to me again, okay, I'll accept that. It's no more than I deserve for having barged into the Golden Duck the other night.

"Hey, there she is," Dustin says.

My eyes fly to the door, expecting to see Jenny walk in, but it isn't her and my brief flare of hope dies away.

"That's *her*," Dustin says excitedly.

"Who?"

"Her sister. Becca."

I look again. The girl, younger than Jenny, wears glasses and has her hair cut short. She heads straight toward the booth of high school girls. I nearly knock over my chair jumping to my feet, but I catch up to her just as she reaches them.

"Hey," I say, "Becca, right? Can I talk to you for a minute?"

The girls in the booth stop talking and stare at me. I ignore them. There was probably a smoother way to do this, but it's too late now.

"I'm Alec, a friend of your sister's," I say hurriedly before she has a chance to tell me to get lost.

"I know who you are," she says. "I saw you at the Duck."

Of course, she did. How many other people saw me make a fool of myself at the Duck? I never should have gone there. Why did that seem like such a good idea at the time? It was one of the worst ideas I've ever had. And I've come up with some doozies.

"It's about Jenny," I say, hoping that will persuade her to give me a few minutes of her time.

She glances at the other girls as if debating whether to join them or talk to me. She shrugs. "Yeah, sure. Why not?"

We walk back to the table I'm sharing with Dustin and have just sat down when April Evans waltzes in with Marcy Harkness. Her eyes slide across us.

"Robbing the cradle, Morrissey?" she says under her breath as they walk past.

I glare after her, but she never looks back.

"Ignore her," Dustin says, taking another bite of his Monster Burger.

"So has there been any word from Jenny?" I ask Becca.

"Nope."

"And you have no idea where she's gone?"

"Nope." Apparently not the chatty type. She stares at me through her glasses. Impossible to know what's going through her head, but I suspect it's not good. I'm the simpleton who thought he could talk her parents into sending Jenny to college after they had decided otherwise.

I wonder how much she knows about Jenny and me. Did Jenny tell her anything about us?

I try again. "Do you think she might be staying with a friend?"

"Like who—Megan Murphy?" There's a hint of sarcasm in her voice. I feel like I'm being judged and found wanting by a freshman girl. Or sophomore. Whatever.

"I already talked to her."

"So did my dad."

"He came to my house too."

"I know."

I get the impression that I'm going to learn nothing from Becca. I might as well have saved myself the embarrassment of approaching her in front of her friends. "You have no idea?"

"Nope."

I haven't given up yet. I glance at Dustin. He's chomping into his Monster Burger and is no help at all. I decide to swallow my pride and ask the question that has been gnawing at me. "Do you know if her disappearance had anything to do with me?"

"Shouldn't I be asking you that question?"

I have the feeling she'd be a good partner on game night. Clearly intelligent, like her sister. Good at counterattack. I might as well be completely honest. What do I have to lose?

"I thought maybe she was mad at me for showing up at the Golden Duck."

"No, I don't think so. Actually, I thought it was sort of cool." She smiles.

I see the resemblance now. She has Jenny's smile.

"But she told me not to."

Becca shrugs. "It's a free world."

"Want a fry?" Dustin asks.

"Why not?" She picks up a fry from his tray and pops it into her mouth.

"You don't seem too upset about the fact that your sister is missing," I tell her, suddenly suspicious.

She shrugs again. "It's not like she was kidnapped. She left a note."

Right. A note for her parents but not for me.

"You must have some idea where she went," I say in a last-ditch effort. "She's your sister."

She studies me from behind her glasses. "Why do you want to know so bad?"

I try to think of a good answer. I can't tell her I'm in love with Jenny when I haven't even told Jenny. And I'm not about to say that in front of Dustin. He'd never let me live it down. I can't say I want to tell Jenny her mother has cancer. If her parents haven't told Jenny, they probably haven't told Becca either. I'll have to be vague.

"I have something important I need to tell her."

"What?" She continues to study me.

I should have known a vague answer wouldn't satisfy her.

"It's personal," Dustin interjects, having polished off his Monster Burger.

"Look, I really want to find her," I say. "Are you sure she didn't leave any clues?"

"Clues? You mean, besides the note?"

Does she have to keep reminding me about the note?

"From what your father said, the note didn't say much."

Becca thinks for a minute. "She took her backpack with her."

So Jenny didn't just rush out of the house. She took something in a backpack. What? Food? Clothes?

"Maybe there's something everyone's overlooked," I suggest.

"Would you like to search her room?" Becca asks.

I'm so surprised by the offer that it takes me a few seconds to respond. "Yeah, sure."

"It's my room too," she explains.

"You'd let me do that?" I ask cautiously, hardly able to believe my luck.

"Sure. Why not?"

I can think of several reasons, top among them her parents might object. Would they want me in their house when they think I may be to blame for Jenny's disappearance? My conscience forces me to ask.

"Well, I'd have to sneak you in," she admits.

I look at Dustin.

"Go for it," he says.

Becca opens the backdoor for me, finger to lips. "Don't make any noise," she whispers. "My mom's lying down."

I assumed her parents would be out, so learning that her mother is at home makes me even more nervous than I already was. How will I explain what I'm doing here if we're caught? I should probably turn around and leave, but instead I skulk after Becca down a hallway to the bedroom she shares with Jenny. Once we're inside, she carefully closes the door. I try to resist the urge to throw it open and run for the nearest exit before Mrs. Chen finds me alone in a bedroom with her underage daughter.

Becca seems oblivious to the risk we're taking.

"This is my side." She waves her hand toward the side of the room where the wall is plastered with posters of animals—

cats, dogs, rabbits, a turtle, elephants, zebras, giraffes, a whale, and more. I'm guessing she likes animals. "And that's Jenny's." She points to the other side. No posters. Just a bulletin board of quotes neatly written out on notecards and postcard pictures of famous scientists like Marie Curie, Albert Einstein, and Stephen Hawking.

"Does she keep a diary?" I ask, thinking a diary might provide clues to where she went. She also might have written about me in it.

"In this family? Are you nuts?"

So no diary. I feel a twinge of disappointment.

"What about the closet? Any clothes missing?"

"Looks the same to me," Becca says, throwing open the door to the closet. "My side." She points to the half that's packed haphazardly with boxes, puzzles, a tennis racket, and a skateboard. "Jenny's side." She points to the neatly organized half. I'm beginning to get the idea. Even their dresser exhibits a split personality—Jenny's side neat and orderly, Becca's a jumble of small objects and a stuffed figure of Totoro.

I sit down on Jenny's side of the bed. *This is where she sleeps*, I tell myself. I feel as if I'm invading her private space. Would she mind me being here?

"See? Nothing," Becca says.

We both look around the room, searching for anything that might reveal where Jenny went. My eyes fall to the floor where the corner of a book peeks out from under the bed. I lean down and pick it up. "What's this?"

"Oh, Jenny likes to read for a while before she turns off her light."

I recognize the book she bought at the Bookery, *Profiles of Women in Science*. Small slips of paper have been inserted to bookmark a few pages.

"Would you mind if I borrowed this?" I ask.

She shrugs. "Why not? You'll bring it back, right?"

"Of course."

"Are you into science too?"

"Not really. How about you?"

"Zoology."

I glance again at the animal posters plastered on the wall on her side of the room. "What do your parents think about that?"

"They say I'll grow out of it."

"Will you?"

"I doubt it."

I have a feeling the Chens have their hands full—two headstrong, ambitious daughters.

"I think I'd better leave before your mother wakes up from her nap. I don't want to get you in trouble."

"Nobody notices what I do. They're too busy worrying about Jenny."

"Well, take advantage of that while you can."

She grins. "Oh, I do."

I drive home with the book on the seat beside me, where I can glance at it from time to time. I can't help wondering if it might hold the answer to Jenny's whereabouts, and even if it doesn't, it's like I have a little piece of Jenny with me.

When I get home, my mother is on her way out to show a house to a client. "There's a letter for you on the kitchen counter," she tells me just before she walks out the door.

I have no idea who would write a letter to me. Curious, I head for the kitchen. I don't recognize the handwriting on the envelope and there's no return address, but the postmark shows it was mailed locally. When I rip it open, I find a note from Jenny. My heart beats faster. She left a note for me after all! My eyes sweep over the neat lines of script.

Dear Alec,

I have to go away for a while. I'm not sure when I'll be back. Please don't think I'm leaving because of you. This has nothing to do with you. I'll explain when I get back.
Love, Jenny

My eyes keep gravitating to the words *Love, Jenny*, then skimming through the note again. She's coming back, but when? And couldn't she have told me where she was going and why? I know no more than I did before. Why all the secrecy?

Well, her note does clear up one thing. She isn't holed up with one of her friends. And she didn't suddenly decide to leave because of me. That's a relief to know.

I charge upstairs to my room with the book and the note, taking the steps two at a time. Since I still have time before I need to report for work, I flip through the pages of the book, pausing on the ones Jenny bookmarked. Most of the women I've never heard of: Lise Meitner, nuclear physicist; Gerty Cori, biochemist; Clara Weisberger, microbiologist. Jenny has underlined several sentences in the chapter on Clara Weisberger. I start reading. When I finish, fine print at the end of the profile catches my eye. She lives in Emmett Falls,

Oregon? Could that be the clue I've been looking for? Would Jenny have gone there to find her? Possibly. In fact, quite likely.

I pace the room, trying to decide what to do. The only way to know if I'm right is to drive there. But when I get off work, it will be too late to drive to Emmett Falls tonight. If I'm right about Jenny going there, how did she manage it? She wouldn't have hitchhiked—too dangerous, not to mention illegal. She must have gone by bus. But I won't be able to check the bus station until tomorrow if I work my shift. Another day lost. I grab my phone and dial Foley's. I tell my supervisor I'm sick. Maybe the flu. It's come on suddenly. There's a moment of silence at the other end of the line, and then a sort of grunt, which I take as permission to stay home.

Ten minutes later I push open the door of the little room downtown that serves as our bus station. Half a dozen people sit on the bolted down plastic chairs with their backpacks and bags beside them. I walk up to the ticket window, where an old man with a mustache blinks at me through his bifocals.

"What can I do for you?"

"I'm looking for this girl." I hold up my phone with the photo I took of us that day on the rocks. "Have you seen her?"

"Why are you looking for her?"

"I'm trying to find her."

"I got that. But *why*?"

"I want to make sure she's okay."

He eyes me narrowly. "How do I know you're not a stalker?"

I stare at him. Do I look like a stalker? But then maybe stalkers don't look any different from everyone else. Would

Jenny consider me a stalker for trying to find her? Maybe I should just wait for her to contact me. But what if she's in trouble? What if she needs me to find her? I hold up my phone again, close to the window, for him to get a good look at the photo.

"Look, I swear I'm not a stalker. Can you just tell me if you've seen this girl?"

"Maybe I have and maybe I haven't, but even if I have—and I'm not saying I have—I couldn't tell you because of confidentiality. Now if you was the police . . . You aren't, are you?"

For a second I'm tempted to say I am. But of course he wouldn't believe me. I shake my head.

"That's what I thought."

I struggle to stay polite. "I just want to know if she was here and bought a ticket to Emmett Falls. Surely you can tell me that much."

He scratches his cheek. "Emmett Falls? What'd you say her name was?"

"Jenny Chen."

He turns to his computer. "And when was this?"

"Yesterday."

"Emmett Falls? Might be I sold a ticket there. I'm not saying I did, but might be."

It had to be Jenny. I could hug him or pump his hand, but he's on the other side of the ticket window, and there's a man standing behind me waiting for his turn, so I just thank him with as much feeling as I can.

"Now you better not make me regret that," he warns.

"You won't," I call over my shoulder as I lunge for the door.

Back in my car, I consider what to do next. I text my mother not to expect me home for dinner and tell her not to worry about me. I could call Jenny's father, but I don't want to get his hopes up. Going to Emmett Falls might be no more than a wild goose chase.

CHAPTER 10

Jenny

Ever since my parents told me I can't start college in the fall, I've felt as if the world is closing in on me. But when I read about Clara Weisberger in that book and learned she lives here in Oregon, it was like a door had been flung open. She is close enough for me to go there and talk to her. Maybe she can even give me advice.

So after breakfast I leave a note for my parents in an envelope in the mailbox so they won't worry, and then I use an ATM machine to withdraw two hundred dollars from my savings account. From there I go straight to the bus station and buy a ticket to Emmett Falls. I have to wait about an hour before it's time to leave, and during that time I worry my parents will find my note and come looking for me. But no one comes, and at last I board the bus along with a dozen other people and it pulls away. I watch the stores, the gas station, the lumberyard, and then the houses slip past the window, and it's as if finally I'm breaking free of Sutter's Bend.

When we are twenty minutes into our journey, I check my phone. I feel guilty when I see the texts from Alec, but I don't answer them. Promising myself that I'll explain everything later, I tuck my phone back in my backpack and turn to the window beside me again to watch the fir trees that line the road rush by and think about what I'll say to Clara Weisberger when we meet.

It's early afternoon when the bus arrives in Emmett Falls, a town not much larger than Sutter's Bend. When I get off the bus with my backpack, it's a warm day with a blue sky overhead. I decide to find a place to grab a bite to eat before trying to track down Clara Weisberger.

After a lunch of soup and a sandwich at a small cafe across the street from the bus stop, I call for a cab and soon find myself in the backseat of a rather beat-up SUV driven by a young bearded driver who likes to talk. It turns out he knows a lot about the town, and when he finds out I've never been here before, he recommends places I should see like a local wine-tasting room and a store where cannabis products are sold, but he's never heard of Clara Weisberger so it's a good thing I looked up her address on the internet. We find her house on a quiet shady street. I ask my driver if he'll wait a few minutes in case I need a ride back since it's possible she's not at home, and even if she is, I can't be sure she'll be willing to talk to me.

I'm nervous walking up the stepping-stone path to the house, uncertain what kind of reception I'll receive. After coming so far, I hope I won't be turned away. The house I'm approaching is a small white house, much like all the others in the neighborhood. Pink azaleas bloom beside the front step, and I hear a woodpecker tapping nearby. I glance back at my ride to summon my courage and then ring the bell. After a minute or two a girl not much older than me answers the door.

She is fair-complexioned with white-blonde hair in a braid and blue eyes that look me over coolly.

"Yes?"

"Is Clara Weisberger at home?" I ask.

"Who wants to know?"

Her aloof manner makes me even more nervous. Apparently she's the gatekeeper. I tell myself she's just doing her job. However, my opportunity to meet Clara Weisberger seems about to slip away, and I don't want to return to Sutter's Bend having achieved nothing.

I give her a big smile. "My name's Jenny Chen. I've just traveled almost two hundred miles to see her."

"Is she expecting you?"

"No, but please, it would mean so much for me to talk to her—five minutes even."

She hesitates, then shrugs. "Wait here. I'll ask her."

The wait is agonizing. To be so close to a famous scientist like Clara Weisberger and yet not able to meet her! Why didn't I explain better to the girl? She may think I'm just a passerby seeking a selfie with a local celebrity.

I glance back again at the SUV waiting patiently by the curb. Why was I so sure that Clara Weisberger would be willing to see me? Why should she? I'm no one. My plan was too impulsive. I didn't think it through.

I'm about to give up and walk back to the SUV when the girl reappears and opens the door for me. "She says you can come in."

I feel a rush of relief and wave my hand at the SUV driver to signal him that he won't need to wait. I can call him later when I'm done.

The girl leads me down a cool dimly lit hall lined with framed photographs of flowers to a room that looks out through sliding glass doors at a garden enclosed by a hedge. Looking out at the garden is a white-haired woman in a wheelchair.

"It's very beautiful, isn't it?" she asks.

"Yes, it is."

"Eve says you want to see me. Is this about the fundraiser?"

"No, I—" I'm suddenly at a loss for words. "I've just come from Sutter's Bend."

"And where is that?"

"On the coast. Not far from Coos Bay."

She's still looking out the window, so I step forward where she can see me. That's when I notice she's blind. Her eyes gaze sightlessly at the garden beyond the windowpanes. She looks like the photograph in my book, only older, probably in her seventies. She has an intelligent face and eyes that crinkle at the corners. There's a faded beauty about her that suggests she was quite attractive when she was younger.

"Eve, would you get us a map, dear?"

The girl, who has been standing behind me, turns and leaves the room without a word.

"Is she your daughter?" I ask.

"No, my daughter is dead. Eve takes care of me."

I feel as if I've said the wrong thing. I should have realized Eve is much too young to be her daughter. Granddaughter maybe but perhaps just a caretaker and no relation at all. Maybe that's what she meant when she said Eve takes care of her.

She gestures toward a nearby wing chair. "Sit down, dear. There's no need for you to keep standing there. You must be tired after your journey."

I perch on the edge of the chair and look around. It's a cheerful room with orange and red accent pillows on a sofa, a tile floor of green and yellow squares, and that wonderful view of the garden through the sliding glass doors.

"That's better," she says after I have sat down. "Now what did you want to ask me? Is this for a school newspaper article or a paper you're writing?"

"No, it's just for me."

"All right. Just for you is a perfectly fine reason."

Her gracious manner makes me feel more confident.

"I read about you in the book *Profiles of Women in Science* and wanted to meet you in person. I thought maybe you could give me some advice."

"Advice about what?"

"I want to be a scientist."

She smiles. "Good for you. The world needs young women interested in a career in the sciences. What field are you interested in, if I may ask?"

"I'm not really sure. Maybe chemistry or physics. I'd like to be able to contribute something to the world, like you have."

"Would you?" She looks amused.

Maybe she sees me as naive. I suppose I am. But this is my chance to get the advice I came for, and I don't want to lose it.

"The problem is my parents want me to be a doctor. But even that's on hold now because they don't have money to send me to college at the same time as my brother. He's in his junior year at the University of Oregon."

"Are you here to ask me for money?"

"Oh, no!" I'm appalled she would think that.

"Good. I'm glad we got that out of the way. Now where is Eve? What's taking her so long to find a map?"

"Shall I go see?"

She dismisses my offer with an impatient wave of her hand. "It's not important. Look—what is your name again?"

"Jenny."

"Jenny, you aren't the first young woman to be told she can't be a scientist, and you won't be the last. Whether it's parents or teachers or well-meaning strangers, people will tell you that you can't do this or you can't do that. You do it anyway. You don't let anyone stop you. It's as simple as that."

She looks like an oracle as she sits there gazing into space, and for a minute I glimpse the young woman she must once have been. I sense granite under that fragile exterior and wonder if it was always there or if it formed over a lifetime. Just being in her presence makes me feel like I could accomplish great things.

"Listen, Jenny," she says. "Life is short. You don't have time to please everyone. You figure out what you want to do and then do it. There's no guarantee that you'll succeed, but if you really want to be a scientist, don't let anyone stand in your way."

She stares unseeing beyond the sliding glass doors at the garden lit by the rays of the afternoon sun. "One by one life has robbed me of everything I hold dear. My husband died. My daughter died. And now I'm blind. But there's one thing it can't take away from me—those years I spent researching and working to understand how a virus replicates. Life is precious.

Time is precious. Don't let yours slip away and wonder later where it went."

"I won't."

"Good."

Eve comes back with a map and spreads it out on a small round wood table, which she moves closer to Clara. After I point out Sutter's Bend, Eve guides Clara's hand to show her the distance I have traveled from Sutter's Bend to Emmett Falls.

"My goodness, you *have* come a long way," says Clara. "Did you drive all that way by yourself?"

"Oh, no, I came by bus."

"And do you have a place to stay for the night?"

"Not yet. But I'm sure I can find someplace in town."

"Nonsense. You should spend the night here with us. It's the least we can do after you've come so far."

"Oh, I couldn't."

"Of course, you could. I insist. We have the space. Eve can fix you up on the sofa. You don't mind sleeping on a sofa, do you?"

"No, of course not."

"Good. Then it's settled."

And just like that I find myself the overnight guest of Clara Weisberger.

While Eve prepares dinner, Clara tells me about her garden. Even though she can't see it, she seems to know all the flowers growing there and where they are. She's particularly proud of her roses. It strikes me as sad that she can't see them.

"I noticed the photos of flowers in the hall," I tell her.

"I took those back when I could still see. Photography was a hobby of mine."

One more thing that blindness has robbed her of. Yet she keeps the photographs on display, so maybe they are still just as important to her as the flowers in her garden.

Before long it's time to eat. Dinner is served in the kitchen at a small table. I didn't realize how hungry I was until I see the bowl of salad on the table and smell the aroma of the chicken with dumplings.

"Cooking is one of Eve's duties, and she's very good at it," Clara says as we begin to eat.

"Have you worked here long?" I ask Eve. We haven't had much chance to talk, and I'd like to get to know her better. There's something guarded about her, as if she's used to keeping people at a distance.

"About a year."

"Eve is an absolute godsend," says Clara. "I don't know how I'd get by without her."

"Oh, you'd hire someone else," Eve says. "But you'd miss my apple strudel. No one else can make apple strudel like mine."

"I'm sure you're right," says Clara. "Your apple strudel is beyond compare."

"Do you live nearby?" I ask Eve.

"I live here."

Again I feel as if I've said the wrong thing. I should have guessed that. Of course, Clara would need round-the-clock care.

"Eve is very good to devote her time to me," says Clara. "I'm afraid I'm poor company. When I was younger, I liked to travel, but now that I can't easily get around, I'm quite the homebody. Eve reads to me or takes me out in the garden. Sometimes we go to hear our local orchestra play in the park."

It's hard to imagine she's famous. She seems so content to live a simple life in an out-of-the-way place without fanfare. On the other hand, I'm surprised someone as young as Eve is satisfied with her job of caretaking an elderly blind woman in a wheelchair.

"Will you go back home tomorrow?" Eve asks me.

Her question catches me off guard because I'm not sure I'm ready to go back to Sutter's Bend. But I don't want them to think I expect to stay longer, so I say, "Yes, of course."

"You seem a bit uncertain," Clara says, immediately picking up on my hesitancy.

"Oh, no. I just have to find out the bus schedule. That's all."

"Well, if you are having second thoughts, you have a night to think about it. I often find that a good night's sleep can give me a new perspective on things."

"Unless you have trouble sleeping," Eve suggests.

"Even then," Clara insists. "Sometimes I've gotten my best ideas tossing and turning in bed. Other times the subconscious can sift through a problem, and when you wake up in the morning, the solution is right there in front of you and you wonder why you never thought of it before."

"I'm sure you're right," I tell her.

Eve watches me across the table with a slightly amused expression but says nothing.

* * *

After dinner we play a game of Parcheesi on the kitchen table with Eve moving Clara's pieces, and by the time the game ends, I have told them about my family and the Golden Duck.

"Surely there's a way for you to go to college," Clara says. "You can't give up. Family is important, but so is your future. If you don't do this, you'll regret it. You'll always wonder what could have been."

"Ah, the *to be or not to be* question," Eve says, deepening her voice for dramatic effect. "It always comes down to that."

"Make fun of me if you wish," Clara retorts, "but you know it's true."

"I know no such thing." Eve consults the clock on the wall. "It's nine."

"Already?" Clara sounds disappointed. "How fast the evening's gone." She turns toward me. "I suppose you're tired after your long journey, dear."

I am, but I wish the evening didn't have to end. "I'm fine—"

"Clara needs her rest," Eve interrupts.

"We are such creatures of habit, Eve and I," Clara says. "You must forgive us. I don't have the energy I once had."

"I'll let you know when the shower's free," Eve tells me as she wheels Clara away.

Left alone, I wander back to the sunroom and sit down on the sofa. Beyond the sliding glass doors, path lights have transformed the garden into a place of enchantment. I close my eyes and my mind drifts. Before long Eve's voice rouses me, letting me know the shower is free. Soon I'm standing under the showerhead in the little bathroom as a warm blast of water courses over me. I feel as if the grime of the day is being washed away and my muscles relax. When I return to the sunroom, Eve has made up the sofa with fresh sheets, a blanket, and a pillow.

"What happened to her daughter?" I ask as I towel dry my hair.

"She committed suicide. Clara's never really gotten over it."

"I didn't know. How old was she?"

"Nineteen."

"How tragic."

"It was a long time ago."

"But still—"

Eve shrugs. "People die. It's sad, but you can't just stop living because other people die."

That's true but to die so young before you've had a chance to live your life seems tragic. I remember what Clara said about making the most of the time you have. Maybe she was thinking of her daughter.

"What about you?" I ask. "Do you have family?"

"A mother."

"Do you see her very often?"

"No. She didn't really want me."

Eve's eyes meet mine evenly. I find it hard to believe a mother would admit such a thing even if it were true.

"Did she say that?"

"More or less."

"Do you have any brothers or sisters?"

"A stepsister. She's still living at home as far as I know."

"And where's home?"

"Vancouver."

"Do you miss it?"

"Sometimes. There's not a lot to do in Emmett Falls."

I can believe that.

"But you're happy here?"

"I suppose so."

"You don't want something more?"

She regards me with those unsettling pale blue eyes. "I'm not like you. I don't have any big plans to change the world."

Her words make me feel guilty. She didn't say it in a mean way—just stated it as a fact. And after all, it's true. I do want to make a difference. But at the same time some part of me wishes I could be more like her. She seems satisfied with what she has. My life would be so much easier if I could be satisfied with what I have. Then maybe I wouldn't chafe at being stuck in Sutter's Bend and having to wait tables at the Golden Duck.

"Do you have a boyfriend?" Eve asks.

"Sort of."

I think of Alec with a twinge of guilt as I remember that I still haven't answered his texts.

"What's he like?"

"He's not really my boyfriend. We've only had one date."

"That's a start. Come on, I want to know all about him. Is he cute?"

"Yes."

She grins. "How did you meet?"

"I've known him since kindergarten."

"Are you in love with him?"

"I don't know. Like I said, we've only had one date."

"Is he a good kisser? Please don't tell me you haven't kissed."

"Yeah, we've kissed." I feel the heat rush to my face.

"Tell me what it was like the first time you kissed."

I hesitate, not wanting to share something so private, but how can I refuse without seeming standoffish?

"He took me to this place by the ocean where there were rocks and boulders."

"Yes?" Eve's eyes light up with anticipation.

"It was night. There was a moon. You could hear the waves breaking on the rocks and the shore. It was like we were all alone in the world, just the two of us."

"Sounds romantic."

"It was. What about you? Have you ever been in love?"

She shrugs. "Several times I thought I was, but it always turned out disappointing. Maybe love's not all it's cracked up to be."

"That sounds cynical."

"Does it? Actually, I think love is the most important thing in a person's life, especially a woman's, don't you?"

Something about the way she says it makes me wonder if she really believes that. It's almost like she said it to test me.

"No, I don't. If being in love meant I'd have to give up my dream of being a scientist, I'm not sure I'd want to fall in love."

She rolls her eyes. "Now you sound like Clara. It's no wonder she ended up all alone. Be careful or that's how you'll end up too. A lonely old woman." She stands up and stretches. "Have you decided what you're going to do tomorrow?"

"What do you mean?"

"Earlier you didn't sound too sure about going home."

"It's just that I was thinking I might go to Eugene and check out the campus. My older brother's there studying premed. I could look him up."

"You should definitely do it. If I were you, I would."

"I don't know. Maybe I should just go home."

"No, go to Eugene. Trust me. I have a feeling about this."

She's so insistent that I have the urge to laugh. But I don't want to offend her. And it would let me postpone a bit longer going back to Sutter's Bend. What would it hurt?

CHAPTER 11

Alec

Of course, I can't just knock on Clara Weisberger's door after dark. She'd probably call the police. And so before I get to Emmett Falls, I stop for the night at a motel. Before turning in, I text my mom and tell her not to worry. I have an idea where Jenny might be and I'm looking into it. When I'm done, I'll be back. I know she won't like it that I've gone in search of Jenny, but I'm not going to let my mother run my life.

The next day the sun is shining when I arrive in Emmett Falls, a sleepy town surrounded by rolling green hills and farmland. By the time I find Clara Weisberger's house, it's almost ten, an hour when I shouldn't catch her still sleeping. I'm so sure this is where Jenny went that when I ring the bell, I half expect her to answer the door. I find myself wondering if she'll be pleased to see me or annoyed. Maybe she'll tell me to go away and leave her alone. Or maybe she'll throw her arms around my neck and kiss me. But it isn't Jenny who answers the door. It's a pale blue-eyed young woman with white-blonde hair who looks quizzically at me.

"May I help you?"

I wonder fleetingly if I got the wrong house.

"Does Clara Weisberger live here?" I ask.

"Maybe." She tilts her head as if studying me. It's disconcerting, to say the least.

Whoever she is, she's much too young to be Clara Weisberger.

"I'm looking for someone."

"Who?"

"A friend of mine. Jenny Chen."

"Oh, you must be Alec."

I feel a wave of relief. So my hunch was right. Jenny came here to seek out Clara Weisberger. My long ride to Emmett Falls was not a wild goose chase after all.

"Is she here?" I ask eagerly.

"Sorry. I'm afraid you've missed her. She left yesterday morning. But come in and maybe we can help you. I'm Eve, by the way."

"Do you know where she's gone?" I ask as I step into a shadowy hallway.

"I'm not sure, but maybe Clara does. And in any case she'll want to meet you. We don't get many visitors."

I follow her to a sunroom that looks out on a garden.

"Jenny didn't say where she was going?"

She shrugs. "Home, I assume."

"She wasn't there when I left."

"Maybe she changed her mind."

If Jenny *is* back in Sutter's Bend, wouldn't she have let me know? Maybe I should have been patient and waited for her to return.

"Wait here," Eve says and leaves me.

I look out at the garden, blooming with flowers, a riot of color, dappled in sunlight. There's a path of stepping stones and a grinning gnome peeking out from under a large green leaf. As I watch, a man who must have been crouching near the gnome suddenly stands. It's startling to see him appear there as if he has materialized out of thin air. He's a young man with a ponytail wearing a T-shirt and jeans. I don't think he sees me watching him from behind the sliding glass doors. Then he crouches down again among the foliage and disappears so completely he might have been a mirage.

I'm still trying to spot him when I hear Eve coming back. She pushes an elderly woman in a wheelchair into the room. I assume this must be Clara Weisberger and then notice her staring eyes and realize with a shock that she's blind.

"Eve tells me you're Jenny's friend and you've come all this way from Sutter's Bend." She holds out her hands to me. When I take them, they feel thin and fragile, her grip as light as a child's.

"I was worried about Jenny."

"And why were you worried about her?"

"I was afraid . . . I mean, she disappeared and no one knew what had happened to her. I found a book she was reading with a page about you bookmarked and thought she might have come here."

"She did, but I'm afraid you missed her."

"That's what I told him," Eve says.

"Did she say where she was going?" I ask.

"I believe she was going home, although I'm not entirely certain. She seemed to have some reservations. Eve, do you know what she decided?"

"No, not really."

"Did she seem okay when she left?" I ask.

"Yes, I think so," the blind woman replies. "Why do you ask?"

"She was upset when she left Sutter's Bend."

"Oh? And why was that?"

I hesitate to say anything Jenny might want kept private, but from the way Clara Weisberger asks, I'm pretty sure she already knows. "Her parents told her they can't afford for her to go to college in the fall, and she was really looking forward to it."

"Yes, she did tell us about that. It's unfortunate. She seems a bright young woman who knows what she wants to do. She just needs to figure out how."

"That's not easy when her parents won't pay for it."

"True, but then she has to work a little harder to make it happen. Life doesn't just hand us what we want on a platter. What about you, young man? Are you going to college?"

"I'm not sure."

"Is money a problem for you too?"

"No, it's not that." I glance at the girl Eve standing beside her watching me with an amused smile. She makes me feel self-conscious. I don't really want to discuss my college plans, or lack of them, but Clara Weisberger apparently has no qualms about asking.

"So why are you unsure about college?"

"I don't think it's for me."

"Well, maybe you're right. College isn't for everyone. So what do you want to do with your life? Have you thought about that?"

"I don't know." I hope she will let the subject drop but she doesn't.

"There must be something you want to do."

I shift uncomfortably. "Look, I should be going."

"But you just got here. Eve, how about a cup of tea for Alec?"

"No, really . . ."

Eve slips away, presumably to make tea. I don't want to be rude, so I resign myself to staying a little longer.

"Do sit down," Clara tells me. "She'll only be a few minutes. Young people are all in such a rush these days."

Reluctantly I seat myself on the sofa with red and orange accent pillows.

"Oh, to be eighteen again!" she says. "That's what you are, right?"

"Yes."

"So young. I remember how it feels. You probably don't think I do at my age, but I do. You feel as if you have all the time in the world." She sighs, and I expect her to tell me how short life is. Do old people really think we don't know that? As soon as Eve brings the tea, I'll drink it and then I'll leave.

"So money isn't an issue," Clara says thoughtfully. "You have parents who will pay for you to go, but you don't want to go."

"They want me to study premed."

"But you don't want to?"

"No."

"Well, there must be other things you could study."

I stay silent. Maybe she will take the hint.

"Did you make low grades?"

"No. It's not that."

"What do your parents think about your not wanting to go? Are they disappointed?"

"They're getting divorced." As soon as I've said it, I feel annoyed with myself for having revealed something I should probably keep private.

"Divorced. Well, they still must have an opinion on the subject."

"My mother thinks I'll come round and my father won't answer my texts. He's in Toronto." I don't mention the girlfriend with the kid. At least I'm showing a little restraint.

"I see. So your life is complicated right now. But you have a choice in front of you."

"A choice my parents want to make for me."

"You must get past that. It's your choice. Are you going to make it for *you* or to spite your parents? No, don't answer that, but think about it. Don't let them push you into making a choice you'll regret, although we all make choices we regret and then can waste years trying to fix them."

I wonder if she's referring to some choice she made that she regrets, but I don't ask. As for me, which choice—going to college or not going—would I most regret?

"I'm not like Jenny. She knows exactly what she wants to do."

"And what does Jenny think you should do?"

"Go to college."

"But of course Jenny can't decide that for you any more than your parents can. You have to ask yourself what *you* want from life."

"That's the thing. I don't know."

She gazes toward the garden. "Everybody has something they want from life. But sometimes it takes a while to figure out what that is. For some it comes easy. Others search all their lives and don't find it. You can spend your whole life focused on your next paycheck or hating your job. But if you're lucky, you find your passion."

Easy for her to say. Maybe not everyone has a passion. Maybe I don't.

Fortunately, before I can say anything else, Eve returns with three cups of tea on a tray.

"Did I miss anything?" she asks brightly.

"Alec was just telling me about his family," Clara says.

To my relief she says nothing about my cluelessness as to what I want to do with my life.

Eve gives me a knowing smile. "Oh? Do you have lots of brothers and sisters?"

What is it about her that makes me so uncomfortable? It's like she's watching me, waiting for me to say or do the wrong thing.

"Just one actually. A younger brother." I take a cup of tea and sip it. I'm not really a tea drinker, but it feels pleasantly warm as it slides down my throat.

Eve snaps her fingers. "I just remembered Jenny told me she might go to Eugene and look up her brother, who's studying there."

Paul. So Jenny may not have gone back to Sutter's Bend after all.

"Is that so?" Clara frowns. "I wonder why she didn't mention it at breakfast."

"Are you sure?" I ask Eve.

"Quite sure."

"Well, now you know where to find her," says Clara. "It seems your trip was not in vain."

"I suppose you'll want to go there," Eve says, sipping her tea and watching me over her cup in that unnerving way she has. I can't make her out. Is she flirting? I look away, not wanting her to think I welcome it.

"Yes."

"In that case maybe you can give me a ride. It just so happens I need to go there to visit a friend."

I nearly choke on my tea. Did she just invite herself along? "I really don't think—"

"What friend?" Clara interrupts. "You never mentioned a friend in Eugene before."

"Didn't I?"

"But what about me? You can't just run off and leave me."

"I'll call the agency and ask them to send someone over."

"Really, Eve."

"It'll only be for a day or two. You'll hardly notice I'm gone."

"Maybe you shouldn't go," I suggest.

"Don't be silly. She'll be fine."

I really don't want to take Eve with me. And I feel guilty taking her away from Clara, but I'm not sure how to refuse without seeming rude. She just assumes I'll agree and ducks out of the room to phone the agency before I can say anything more.

It means waiting another hour for a replacement caretaker to arrive. I don't think Clara is happy about the situation, but she seems resigned to it. In the end I don't have much choice but to let Eve tag along.

CHAPTER 12

Jenny

It's around noon when I arrive in Eugene. From the bus station I take a cab to the university, and with the help of a map on my phone, I soon find my way to Paul's dorm.

At the desk in the lobby I explain that I'm looking for my brother, Paul Chen.

The girl at the desk, who's wearing black lipstick and has a piercing in one eyebrow, consults her computer. "Sorry. There's no one by that name here."

"There has to be."

She looks again. "Sorry. No."

I have his cell number and could phone him, but I was hoping to surprise him. I wonder why he isn't in her database? I'm sure it's the right dorm. If he's in the same room he used to be, he's in 312.

Since there's an elevator nearby, I decide to go up and see if he's there. When I reach the third floor, I get off the elevator as a couple of guys get on. They don't seem to think it's unusual to see a girl on this floor, so that makes me feel a little more confident when I knock on the door to room 312.

A guy with rumpled hair and a bare chest opens the door. "Yeah?"

"Does Paul Chen live here?" I ask, wondering if this is his roommate. It's hard to imagine my obsessively neat brother living with a roommate who looks like he considers clothes optional.

"Who wants to know?"

"His sister."

"Sorry. You got the wrong room." He starts to shut the door.

"Hey, wait," says a male voice in the background. "He used to live here but he moved."

"Do you know where he moved?" I ask, raising my voice.

"Aldergate Terrace."

"Is that in walking distance?"

He comes to the door. Dark eyes, wiry. "I can give you a ride if you want. I was just about to go out."

It's nice of him to offer, and if Aldergate Terrace is far enough away to require a ride, I should probably accept.

"Thanks. That would be great."

I'm sure my mother would not approve if she knew I had just accepted a ride from a stranger. Even worse, it turns out to be on the back of a motorcycle. But I gamely wrap my arms around his waist, and by the time we reach our destination, I'm grateful he offered the ride because I would not have wanted to walk so far.

Aldergate Terrace is a two-story multi-unit apartment building with a neatly manicured lawn and a couple of oak trees. Looking up at the building after my good Samaritan has roared off on his motorcycle, I wonder how long Paul has been living off-campus. I'll bet my mom wouldn't approve of that either. I could call him on my phone to let him know I'm standing outside, but when I notice mailboxes with names and find his unit number, I decide to stick to my original plan of surprising him. Since he has an outside door on the second-floor landing, all I have to do is climb the stairs and ring his bell.

On the second ring Paul answers the door and stares at me in disbelief. "Jenny, what are you doing here? How did you get here?"

"Who is it?" someone in the background calls.

"Aren't you going to invite me in?" I ask.

"What are you doing here?" he repeats, glancing beyond me down the landing as if expecting to see Mom or Dad there. "Are you alone?"

I don't understand why he doesn't invite me in. "Yes, I'm alone. I just came from your dorm. When did you move off-campus?"

He looks toward the street as if something has just caught his attention. "A couple of months ago."

I see his roommate now, who has come up behind him. Tall, glasses, nerdy looking. He smiles at me.

"This is Nathan," my brother says. "Nathan, my sister Jenny."

"The brainy one, right?"

"They're both brainy."

He holds the door open, and I step inside. It's a very small apartment with one room serving as living room and kitchen.

Paul scoops up some magazines and looks around the room with a frown. It's really not messy. "So you want something to drink? Water? Soda? Tea?" If they drink something stronger, he's not offering me any.

"Water."

He strides to the sink in the little kitchen, fills a glass with water, and then hands it to me. "Nothing's wrong at home, is it?"

"No, I just thought I'd come take a look at the college."

"Why? You'll be here soon."

He doesn't know?

"You know Mom and Dad changed their mind about me going to college in the fall, right?"

He looks shocked. "You're kidding. Why would they do that?"

"They say there's not enough money to send us both."

"Oh, Jenny. I'm so sorry. No, I didn't know."

I wonder when they were planning to tell him. Maybe they didn't want him to feel guilty about it.

"What are you going to do?" he asks.

"Well, there's not much I can do."

"So you're going to stay in Sutter's Bend and work at the Golden Duck?"

"What choice do I have?"

"Geez, Jenny, there must be some way for you to go. Mom and Dad always wanted you to go."

"I guess they changed their mind."

"I'm sure they'd send you if they could."

I drop my backpack on a chair. Paul stares at it as if noticing it for the first time.

"So how did you get here?"

"By bus."

His eyes narrow. "Do Mom and Dad know you're here?"

"Not exactly."

"What do you mean, not exactly? Have you run away from home?"

"You make it sound like I'm ten years old."

"Jenny, you have to let them know where you are. They'll be worried sick."

"I left a note."

"I think I'll just leave you two alone a minute to sort things out," Nathan says and ducks into a doorway leading to the next room.

"You have to phone them," Paul says.

"All right. I'll phone them. Just as soon as I've decided what I'm going to do."

"Where will you stay?"

I look at his sofa. "I was sort of hoping I could stay with you for a couple of days."

His eyes fly to the doorway through which Nathan has disappeared. "There's just the sofa. I don't think—"

"The sofa will be fine. I'd even settle for the floor."

"I don't know. I really should call Mom and Dad and let them know you're here."

"Are you going to tell them you're living off-campus?"

His silence tells me what I suspected. He doesn't want them to know.

"It's just for a couple of days."

Yes, it's an imposition, showing up out of nowhere and asking to crash on his sofa. It's a small apartment, barely larger than a dorm room. How was I supposed to know he'd moved off-campus? I thought maybe some girls in his dorm might give me floor space to sleep on for a couple of nights.

"Will your roommate mind?" I glance at the doorway where Nathan vanished. It occurs to me that there is probably only one bedroom—a very small one at that—and I realize my brother has another secret he's keeping from our parents.

CHAPTER 13

Alec

We're hardly out of Emmett Falls when Eve turns on the radio and starts searching for a station with music she likes. When nothing appeals to her, she gives up and flips it off with a sigh. After driving all the way from Sutter's Bend on my own, it feels odd to have someone sitting beside me in my Camaro. She's wearing sunglasses, a white T-shirt, and jeans. Up close she seems younger. I wonder how old she is but don't want to ask because I don't want her to think I'm interested. I feel as if she took advantage when she invited herself along. Clara too seemed taken aback by her sudden decision to go to Eugene with me. I wish now I had refused to let her come along.

"Will she be okay?" I ask.

"Clara? Yes, of course. It does us both good to spend some time apart. Too much of another person is wearing, don't you think?"

"It depends on the other person."

"Don't worry about Clara. She'll be fine."

Maybe so, but I still don't feel right about it.

"Do you like working for her?"

"It's okay."

"You don't sound too enthused."

"Well, sometimes it gets a little monotonous. You know? The same thing day after day. I suppose when you're seventy-eight years old and stuck in a wheelchair, that's okay, but for me it gets to be a bit of a bore."

"Have you thought about getting another job?"

"I'm sure eventually I will. In the meantime I'm saving up my money."

"For anything in particular?"

"I haven't decided. Maybe I'll go to Venice for Carnival next year. I think that would be fun."

"Have you been abroad before?"

"I've been to Burning Man."

"Oh, yeah? What's it like?" I don't point out that Burning Man isn't abroad; it's in Nevada.

"Oh, you know. People in costumes. Lots of music. Art installations. Light shows. Lots of weed and meth. And dust! Oh my god, the dust! It's everywhere. It coats your skin, it gets in your eyes and your hair and your lungs. But no one cares. They're too busy partying."

I glance at her. In spite of her impulsiveness, she doesn't seem the type for a scene like she described. She seems more like a loner.

"What?"

"Nothing."

"You should go sometime. You might like it."

I doubt that but keep it to myself. "Are you from around here?"

"Vancouver."

"Is your family there?"

"No, they're all dead."

I glance at her again. "I'm sorry. What happened?"

"A car accident. It was sleeting and their car went off a bridge. It was in all the newspapers. I was lucky I wasn't with them. I had to stay home that day with a babysitter because I had a cold. My aunt took me in after my family died. I was ten."

"That's awful."

She shrugs. "It was a long time ago."

I try to change the topic. "Have you worked for Mrs. Weisberger for very long?"

"About a year. How long have you and Jenny been together?"

"Not very long."

"You must really like her, coming all this way to find her."

"Yeah, I do."

"I'm surprised she didn't tell you where she was going."

"I'm sure she has her reasons."

"I suppose. But if *I* had a boyfriend, I don't think I'd just take off and not tell him where I was going."

I don't like her implied criticism of Jenny. "She was upset."

"I suppose so." She sounds doubtful.

I try to change the subject again. "So you have a friend in Eugene?"

"Several friends actually."

"Do your friends know you're coming?"

"No, but it's not a problem."

"Do they attend University of Oregon?"

"Does it matter?"

"No, of course not. I was just wondering."

We lapse into silence then, which is fine with me. Eve tries again to find music on the radio and again gives up.

"Do you know much about Clara?" she asks when another five minutes have passed.

"Just what I read in that book." I nod over my shoulder at Jenny's book lying in the back seat.

She glances back at it disinterestedly. "Do you know anything about her marriage?"

"Like what?"

"It was pretty rocky. She was married to her research. It came before everything else, including her family."

I wonder why she's telling me this. "So?"

"So I'm saying maybe you should be careful about Jenny."

"Jenny isn't Clara. They're totally different people."

"Are they? Listen, I'm just saying you might want to think twice about what it could be like to be married to someone who wants to be a famous scientist."

"Who said anything about marriage?"

"Women like that don't make good wives or mothers."

I wonder where this is coming from. Did she take a dislike to Jenny? Does she hold a grudge against Clara? Or does she disapprove of women scientists in general? I don't ask. It's not a topic I want to pursue with her. And my relationship with Jenny is my business.

At least when we get to Eugene, I'll be rid of her. We'll go our separate ways, and she can find her own way back to

Emmett Falls. After all, I never agreed to give her a roundtrip ride. Once I find Jenny, we'll head back to Sutter's Bend. Regardless of why she took off, I'm sure she'll want to go home when she hears her mother has cancer.

"What are you thinking about?" Eve asks. "You've hardly said a word for the last ten minutes."

"I was just wondering how to find Jenny when we get there."

"Simple. Find her brother."

"And how do I do that?"

"Leave it to me. I'm good at finding people." She pulls out her phone and starts searching the internet.

By the time we get to the outskirts of Eugene, she has an address.

"And where do you want me to drop you?" I ask.

"First let me help you find her brother."

"It's not necessary. I have the address now."

"Oh, but I want to."

It doesn't seem worth arguing with her since I won't have to put up with her much longer. GPS guides us to Aldergate Terrace, a sprawling brick building with a few shade trees and a green freshly mowed lawn. After we get out, we find Paul's last name and apartment number on one of the mailboxes near the stairs that lead to the next level, so we are in the right place. I'd prefer for Eve to wait in the car, but of course she insists on climbing to the second floor with me.

Paul answers the door and looks from me to Eve. He doesn't seem to recognize me. "Can I help you?"

"We're looking for Jenny," I tell him.

"Jenny?"

"Your sister."

"And who might you be?" He looks me over.

"Alec Morrissey. I'm a friend of Jenny's."

"I don't think I've heard her mention you."

His studied indifference is beginning to irritate me. "Look, is she here or not?"

"Well, no. I assume she's in Sutter's Bend."

He recognizes me or he wouldn't have mentioned Sutter's Bend.

"I just came from there."

"Well, then I don't know where she is."

I can tell by the way he looks away that he's not being truthful. Is Jenny inside? Impossible to tell since he's standing in front of the door blocking our view of the interior of the apartment.

"It's really important for me to find her," I tell him. "I have a message for her."

"You can give it to me."

"I have to give it to her in person."

He looks at Eve. "Are you a friend of Jenny's too?"

"Like sisters," she says, crossing her fingers.

He looks skeptical. In another minute he'll close the door in our faces. I'd better talk fast if I want to find out what he knows about Jenny's whereabouts.

"Look, do you have any idea where she might be? We're pretty sure she's not back in Sutter's Bend."

"Sorry. If she's not there, I have no idea where she is."

I'd like to push past him into the apartment to see if she's there, but of course that's out of the question. I've already made a bad impression on her parents. I don't want to make an enemy of her brother.

"If you see her, will you tell her I'm looking for her? Tell her it's important."

"Of course."

He doesn't smile. I can't tell what's going through his mind. Will he give her my message?

"Tell her to call me. Or text me."

"Okay."

He retreats inside, and we are left facing the closed door.

"Well, that wasn't very helpful," Eve says.

"I think he knows where Jenny is."

"Yeah, I kind of got that impression too. So what do we do now?"

"I'll drop you at your friends'."

"And then what?"

"I don't know. I haven't decided."

"Are you going back to Sutter's Bend?"

"Not tonight. It's too far and I want to find Jenny first."

"Are you giving up so easy?" she asks as we start back down the stairs.

The question irritates me, as she no doubt intended it to. She seems to know exactly what to say to get under my skin.

"What do you suggest?"

She grins. "We could stake out the building and see if she turns up."

I picture us sitting for hours in the Camaro waiting for Jenny to appear. I would have to endure more of Eve's annoying questions and innuendoes.

"*We* are doing nothing of the kind. Now where should I drop you?"

By now we have reached the car. Eve rummages in her pocketbook. I expect her to pull out her phone and give me an address where I can drop her, but instead she stops rummaging and looks at a sparrow on the lawn pecking for bugs or seeds, then up at the sky, and then at me. She sighs.

"I have a confession to make."

"What?"

"I don't actually know anyone here."

She lied when she said she had friends in Eugene? Why did I not guess that? And if she has no friends here, why did she insist on coming? I feel as if I've been duped.

She tries to look contrite. "Don't be mad. I want to help you find Jenny."

"When were you planning to tell me you have no friends here?"

"When I had to. Which I just did."

I look around at the freshly clipped grass and the stone engraved with the name Aldergate Terrace. "I should leave you here. It would serve you right."

"But you won't. It wouldn't be safe. I could be mugged. Or raped. You wouldn't want that to happen, would you?"

I'm sorely tempted to just leave her, but she's right. It'll soon be dark. If something happened to her, it would be my fault.

"So are we going to stake out the place?" she asks.

"No, we are not."

"What then?"

"I suppose we'll have to find someplace to eat."

"Oh, goody. I wasn't going to mention it, but I am getting sort of hungry. I saw some eating places downtown. There was this place with a red awning . . ."

I had expected to find Jenny before dark and start back to Sutter's Bend. Now it's clear I'll have to spend the night in Eugene and continue my search for her in the morning. The question is what to do with Eve. I suppose I have no choice but to make sure she has a place to stay for the night, but I'm not going to pay for a motel room for her. If she wants her own room, she'll have to pay for it herself.

When I tell her, she says, "That's okay. I can share your room. Or if you're sleeping in your car, I can too. In fact, it might be fun."

It would most definitely not be fun. In fact, the one thing I can think of worse than sharing a motel room with Eve would be sleeping in the Camaro with her. Not only would it be tight quarters but we'd also probably get cited by the police.

I start the engine. Okay. Time to look for a motel. If I have to share a room with her, so be it. I suspect she doesn't have much money with her, if any at all, which means I'll also have to drive her back to Emmett Falls tomorrow or pay for her bus fare. I grit my teeth. Too bad I didn't have the guts to say no when she asked to come to Eugene with me.

After we eat at a small pizzeria near the university, I rent a room with two beds at a budget motel near the airport. While Eve showers, I text Jenny and tell her I'm in Eugene. *If you are here, can we meet?* Then I try calling my father again, but he's still not answering his phone.

I'm sitting on the bed staring at my phone when Eve emerges from her shower wrapped in a towel, her hair loose and damp.

"Texting Jenny?" she asks.

"Maybe."

She juts out her lower lip, pretending to pout. "You aren't still mad at me, are you? Look, it's hard to take care of an old lady, no matter how famous she is. It's like life is passing me by, and sometimes I get the urge to be part of it. Can you blame me for wanting to have a little fun?"

I hardly see how the long drive from Emmett Falls could be considered fun, but taking care of an old lady in a wheelchair probably *is* boring. Maybe I was too quick to judge her. All the same, I don't think I should feel obligated to drive her back to Emmett Falls. Tomorrow I'll buy her a bus ticket and be done with her.

I take my turn in the shower then and under the hot spray of the showerhead start to feel better. When I come back, Eve has turned out the light by her bed. She's facing the wall, the blanket wrapped around her, shoulders and back bare. Is she sleeping in the nude? I tell myself to think about something else. The sooner she's on a bus on her way back to Emmett Falls, the better.

CHAPTER 14

Jenny

Look, I can't promise you anything, but here's what I can do," the woman behind the desk says. "I'll take a closer look at your application and see if we can offer you any more financial aid. You also might be able to find work off-campus. We have some computers in the next room which you're welcome to use to search local job listings. Maybe you'll be able to find something that would help pay your way."

I thank her and, feeling encouraged, take a look at the listings on the computers in the next room. If I find a job, maybe I can stay in Eugene and not go back to Sutter's Bend. I know my parents would like me to continue working at the Duck, but they could hire someone to take my place. They can't expect me to stay there forever.

After finding several leads, I call and set up interviews for later in the day. The jobs are all part-time and don't pay much, but I feel elated. Maybe I can find a way to start college in the fall after all.

With a few hours free before my first interview, I decide to check out the buildings where science classes are taught. I pull up a map of the campus on my phone and head first to Klamath Hall, a plain rectangular building where the chemistry department is located. When I get there, I wander from floor to floor peering into classrooms. Finding an empty lab, I slip inside to take a closer look. The room smells faintly of acetone. Neat rows of lab tables with stools line the room. Against one wall is a cabinet containing beakers, flasks, test tubes, Bunsen burners, and other lab equipment. Scrawled on the blackboard is an equation, half erased. I run my hand along the smooth black surface of a table and imagine what it would be like to take a class in this room. From the window I can see students with backpacks strolling the walkways and a red-brick building surrounded by green grass—Willamette Hall, home to the physics department and the next building I plan to check out.

"May I help you?" asks a young man in glasses from the doorway. Tall, slim, academic-looking. He looks a little old to be a student but young for a professor. No tie, but his shirt and jeans could signify he's either.

I feel embarrassed to have been caught exploring the lab. "I was just looking."

"It's a nice view, isn't it? Are you a student here?"

"No, but I hope to be soon."

"So you're checking out the campus?"

"Yes."

"Would you like a quick tour of the building? I could show you around."

"Oh, I wouldn't want to take your time."

"Not a problem." He glances at his watch. "I just finished a class, and it so happens I have the next hour free."

I can't think of any reason not to accept his invitation, and I'd really like to see more of the building, so I accept his offer.

"By the way, I'm Malcolm Whitmore," he says as we start down the hall. "And you are?"

"Jenny Chen."

"Jenny. I like that. It suits you. And so if you'll come with me, Jenny Chen, I'll show you some of the many wonders that await you in the science department at University of Oregon. Have you decided what you'll major in?"

"I'm not sure. Chemistry, or maybe physics."

"Well, you're in the right place."

"Are you a professor?"

He grimaces. "Sorry, no. Just a lowly grad assistant."

I relax a bit. At least he isn't a professor. A grad assistant doesn't seem nearly as intimidating, even if he's older than me.

And so for the next half hour he guides me through a dozen or more classrooms and labs, shows me a large lecture hall, and introduces me to a couple of professors sitting in their offices and several students roaming the halls. Afterward, we go to a nearby cafeteria, where he buys me an egg salad sandwich with a pickle for lunch and we talk about some of the latest research being done in gene editing with CRISPR technology, which he's interested in.

In fact, we get so caught up in our conversation, I wonder if he's forgotten he has only an hour free. He seems in no rush to leave. Not that I mind. I like having the opportunity to talk to someone else interested in science. He makes me feel as if wanting to study science is the most natural thing in the world instead of odd. It's like we speak the same language. I no longer feel weird because I'm interested in science, as I did in high school.

Finally he notices the time. "Oh, crap. I have to run. I have a class to teach. Would you like to sit in?"

I remember the appointments I made earlier and tell him I can't.

"Dinner then?"

As much as I like talking to him about science, I'm not sure I want to go out to dinner with him. But I also don't want to cause any ill feelings with the first person I've met at the university who shares my interests.

"Oh, come on. You have to eat. Why not with me? I know this little place . . ."

I laugh. It's hard to say no to him, and the prospect of having more time to continue our conversation is tempting. At the same time I'm nervous about going out with someone older who I hardly know. But he may be able to give me some good advice, I tell myself. And it's kind of flattering to think a grad student would find me interesting.

So I agree to have dinner with him. I tell myself it's not really a date. It's just dinner.

Before we go our separate ways, I give him my phone number and Paul's address, cringing at the thought of what my brother will say when he finds out I'm having dinner with a grad student.

Then I trek downtown to interview for a job waiting tables at a cafe. At least this is something I know I can do. But when I get there, the manager seems unimpressed by my experience at the Golden Duck. She says she will think about it and get back to me. The next interview involves working with a team of workers at a pizzeria. Here too the owner is noncommittal, saying he has more interviews to do before he decides who he will hire. Two more interviews are equally disappointing. By the time I return to Aldergate Terrace, I'm feeling discouraged.

"None of these jobs would pay enough for you to cover rent for a room," Paul declares when I tell him about my interviews.

It doesn't seem like a good time to mention Malcolm, but in a few hours he'll pick me up for our dinner date so I have to tell Paul about him. As I expected, my brother objects.

"Let me get this straight," he says, pacing between the table and the door, a distance of barely half a dozen steps in the close quarters of the little apartment. "You met some guy—someone you don't know—and agreed to go out to dinner with him?"

I wish now I hadn't agreed to go to dinner with Malcolm, but I did. It's too late to change my mind. I have to go through with it. If only Paul wouldn't make such a big deal of it.

"Hold on a minute," Nathan says from the sofa as he pushes up his glasses and prepares to bite into an apple. "Isn't she old enough to make up her own mind?"

I glance at him gratefully. I like Nathan.

"You don't understand," Paul says, wheeling on him. "If our parents find out, they'll blame me. They'll say I should have stopped her. I'm her brother. I'm supposed to look out for her."

"Don't you think she can look out for herself?"

Thank you, Nathan!

Paul paces some more. "What if he takes advantage of her?"

"He's not going to take advantage of me," I say.

"You can't know that. And what about Glen?"

"We broke up."

He stops pacing and stares at me. "Since when?"

"Since about a week ago."

"You're serious? You and Glen broke up?"

It's almost comical how shocked he looks. You'd think I just announced I was shaving my head or getting a swastika tattooed on my forehead.

"Who's Glen?" Nathan asks.

"Practically a member of our family," Paul mutters as he resumes pacing. "Do Mom and Dad know you broke up?"

"Yes, of course they know."

He stops again. "Does that have something to do with your sudden decision to leave Sutter's Bend?"

"No, it has nothing to do with my decision to leave. I told you. Mom and Dad say they can't afford for me to come here. I couldn't bear the idea of staying in Sutter's Bend and waiting tables at the Golden Duck for the rest of my life."

"It wouldn't be the rest of your life—just until they could afford it."

"And when would that be? It might be never."

"Please," Nathan says, "let's all take a deep breath before anyone says something they'll regret."

Paul and I glare at each other. Then he goes into the kitchen and bangs around noisily with the pots and pans, taking out his anger on them. I retreat to the bathroom to change into my better blouse for the date.

He's still not speaking to me when Malcolm arrives to pick me up. I'm watching out the window for Malcolm, and when I see him climbing out of a car in the parking lot, I dash out the door to avoid awkward introductions.

Paul's disapproval has added to my qualms about my date with Malcolm. As soon as I slide into the car beside him, I feel twinges of panic. It's only dinner, I remind myself again.

We eat at an Italian restaurant on East Broadway. Over pasta and red wine, he tells me about his graduate research project involving fruit flies and gene editing.

"But what I'd really like to work on is telomeres," he confesses. "Just think what it could mean for the future if we could discover how to keep our telomeres from shortening. Longer lives. Who knows how long we could live? Seriously. You should think about going into telomere research."

"Maybe I will."

"Here's the thing." He leans forward, elbows on the table. "I might be able to get you on my team. The fruit fly project, I mean. Nothing major, of course, but assistants are always needed—if you'd be interested in that."

"I would," I say quickly, hardly able to believe I just got offered an opportunity to work on a graduate science project when I'm not even a first-year student yet. I wonder if it would be as a volunteer or if I could get paid but don't want to seem money-grubbing by asking. Even if I didn't get paid, it would still look good on my resume.

"Great. And down the line, who knows, maybe there will be other projects. Something tells me we'd make a great team."

I feel my face grow warm. I can't help thinking of Pierre and Marie Curie. Maybe this is one of those meetings destined to be the stuff of legends. Now I'm glad I came. It seems silly of me to have worried whether I should come.

He tells me more about telomeres and mutant fruit flies as we work through our pasta entrees.

"Hey, how about we go back to my place?" he asks when we're waiting for the tab.

I can hear Paul's voice in my head. *You don't know him.*

Malcolm notices my hesitation. "Am I moving too fast? Sorry. It's just that I have a feeling we're a lot alike."

I do too. So why do I feel so uneasy about his suggestion to go back to his place? Maybe because I can't be sure what that might entail. "I think I should get back. My brother will worry."

"Your brother?" His eyebrows raise.

I shouldn't have mentioned Paul. I sound like I'm still in high school. Hurriedly I try to make light of it.

"Yeah, you know how big brothers are."

"Maybe if he met me?" He watches me through his glasses.

I could tell him it would make no difference, but fortunately I'm spared having to answer by the arrival of the waitress with our tab.

When we pull up to the curb in front of Aldergate Terrace, I reach for the door handle, relieved the evening is over.

"Don't I get to walk you to the door?" he asks, his smile twitching nervously.

"Maybe it's better if we say goodnight here," I suggest, just in case Paul might throw open the door when we got there.

"Well, do I at least get a goodnight kiss?"

"Maybe next time."

I hop out of the car before he has time to say anything else and wonder as I hurry toward the stairs that lead up to Paul's apartment if I just blew my opportunity to work with Malcolm on his project.

Why did he have to make everything seem so awkward? Or maybe he didn't. Maybe it was my fault for failing to see that he was hoping for more than just dinner.

When I walk in, Nathan is watching TV in the semi-dark while Paul pores over a textbook at the table by the light of a small high-intensity lamp. Paul doesn't bother to look up. He must still be miffed at me.

"How'd it go?" Nathan asks, as if to make up for my brother's frosty reception.

"Good."

"Someone was here looking for you."

"Who?"

He looks at Paul.

"Alec Morrissey," Paul says, still without looking up.

My stomach does a flip. "Alec was here?"

"Yes."

"What did he want?"

Now Paul looks up, an aggrieved expression on his face. "He said he had a message for you. Apparently he's been trying to contact you."

I think of the missed phone calls and the texts I haven't read. I had tried to push them out of my mind, telling myself I would get to them later. How did Alec find me anyway? No one knew I was coming here.

"Did he say what the message was?"

"No, but he said it's important."

He probably said that so I would call him back.

"Who's Alec?" Nathan asks.

"A friend."

He raises his eyebrows but doesn't pursue it.

"The question is, why is Alec Morrissey looking for you?" Paul says. "And since when have the two of you been so chummy?"

"For a while."

"Oh, and he had a girl with him."

I try to hide my surprise. I don't want to give Paul the satisfaction of having caught me off guard.

Could Alec be back together with April Evans? Would she have been willing to come such a long distance with him to bring me a message? But if not April, then who?

"Did you tell him I'm here?"

"You said, *tell no one*, so I denied I'd seen you. But I don't think he believed me."

I wonder what could be so important that Alec would drive all the way from Sutter's Bend to find me. I should have explained before I left. I think of how we sat on that boulder by the water and talked, and how my heart pounded when we kissed. I shouldn't have just disappeared. I owe him an explanation.

CHAPTER 15

Alec

Jenny's text says she will be at the Pancake House on East Broadway at nine if I want to meet. After reading it, I rush about the motel room, urging Eve to get up and get ready to leave. She groans but tumbles out of bed and starts pulling on clothes.

Since we have to check out of the motel, I have little choice but to take her with me to the Pancake House. We are sitting across from each other in a booth when Jenny walks in. She stops, a look of surprise on her face when she sees Eve, who smiles and waves as if they are good friends.

I assume Jenny will slide into the booth beside me, but instead she slides in beside Eve. I try not to take this as a bad sign, but my confidence wavers. I face them both across the table, feeling outnumbered.

Jenny glances sideways at Eve. "What are you doing here?"

"Keeping Alec company, of course." Eve winks at me.

"She insisted on coming along," I tell Jenny, not wanting her to think I invited Eve to come with me to Eugene.

Eve rolls her eyes.

131

"But how did you two . . . ? You went to Emmett Falls?"

I nod. "I thought you might have gone there. Your sister showed me that book of profiles of women scientists. In fact, I brought it with me. It's in my car."

"Oh."

That *oh* makes me feel even more uneasy. If only Eve were not here. There's so much I want to say to Jenny, so many questions I want to ask, but not with Eve listening in and smirking.

"Why did you leave?" I ask Jenny.

"I couldn't stay."

That tells me nothing. I still want to know if it was because of me. I search her eyes for the truth, but she looks away. "You didn't answer my texts." It comes out sounding like an accusation, but that wasn't how I meant it.

"I'm sorry."

"Well, now that we've gotten that out of the way, can we order?" Eve asks, looking about. "I'm hungry." She waves to catch the attention of a waitress rushing by. The harried-looking young woman skids to a halt and whips out a small pad to take our order. This done, she hurries on to another customer. Jenny's eyes meet mine again. I want to reach across the table and hold her hand, but Eve's presence makes me self-conscious.

"You told Paul you have a message for me?" Jenny asks.

"Yes. From your father."

"What is it?"

I glance at Eve. She smiles brightly and leans forward, all ears. "Your mother's sick. They want you to come home."

Jenny frowns. "What do you mean—*sick*?"

"She has cancer." It sounds wrong to put it so bluntly.

"Cancer? Are you sure? They're not just saying that to get me to come home?"

"No, I don't think so. Why would they make up something like that?"

"You never know," Eve says with a shrug. "Parents can be devious."

Jenny bites her lip, which I notice she does when she's feeling anxious.

Before Eve and I got to Eugene, I worried that I wouldn't find Jenny, but it never occurred to me that she might refuse to go back to Sutter's Bend.

"Just give me a minute," she says, sliding out of the booth.

I watch her walk away, fumbling in her bag for her phone. She goes outside for privacy. Through the window we see her pacing on the sidewalk, her phone pressed to her ear. I want to run outside and be with her, but I stay where I am. I need to let her have her space.

"You know it'll never work out," Eve says.

"What won't?"

"You and Jenny."

"Why not?"

"You're too different."

I'm not going to argue with her. She wants me to doubt myself. I'm not sure why. Maybe she gets some kind of pleasure out of tormenting me. She's been a thorn in my side since we left Emmett Falls.

"Why did you come along anyway?" I ask her.

"I suppose I was bored."

We watch Jenny out the window. I expect she's calling home to see if what I told her about her mother is true. Impossible to guess from her expression how the conversation is going.

"You and I have much more in common than you and Jenny," Eve says.

"You know nothing about me."

"Oh, but I do. I know your parents are getting divorced."

She must have heard me tell Clara that.

Eve smiles, satisfied that she has gotten under my skin again.

"It's none of your business."

"Oo, touchy."

Beyond the window Jenny has finished her phone call. She looks at the street and the cars zipping by. Then she squares her shoulders and marches back in.

"Everything okay?" I ask when she slides back into the booth beside Eve.

"You were right. She has cancer. They're going to start chemo." She swallows hard. "I should go home."

"I'll take you."

"What about Eve?" She glances at Eve beside her.

"We can drop her at the bus station. She can take the bus back to Emmett Falls."

"*What?*" Eve says. "You can't just dump me like I'm a stray cat you're getting rid of."

"Or you could stay here in Eugene if you'd prefer."

"I don't know anybody here!"

"You should have thought of that sooner."

Her lip trembles. Just as the waitress arrives with our pancakes, she starts crying. The waitress tries not to notice. Jenny puts her arm around Eve and throws me a look of reproach. "Of course we'll take you back to Emmett Falls."

I could point out that going back to Emmett Falls will mean not getting back to Sutter's Bend until well after dark, but I doubt it will do any good. I have a feeling Jenny's mind is made up. I'll just have to endure another road trip with Eve. At least this time Jenny will be along and I won't have to be alone with Eve.

But before we can leave Eugene, we have to return to Aldergate Terrace to let Paul know what's happening. He's just as shocked to learn that his mother has cancer as Jenny was.

"Of course you have to go back," he tells her. "If it weren't for my classes, I'd go home too."

"I can't believe they didn't tell us," she says.

Eve, who asked to use the bathroom, comes back. "What's the rent on a place like this?"

Paul gives her a blank stare. "I didn't quite catch who you are. How exactly does Jenny know you?"

"I met her when I was in Emmett Falls," Jenny snaps. "Honestly, Paul, you're embarrassing me. She's my friend."

Eve perches on a dining chair, which is about the only unoccupied place to sit in the small apartment. "It's okay. He's just being big brotherly. I understand."

"Would anybody like a glass of lemonade?" Nathan asks.

"We should probably be going," I say.

Jenny stands up and pulls on her backpack.

"Phone me," Paul tells her. "Let me know how she is."

* * *

Soon we're on the road, the rolling countryside and stands of fir trees rushing by, each of us lost in our own thoughts. Eve curls up on the backseat and falls asleep. Jenny reads her book about women scientists. I'd like to talk, but she seems engrossed in her book, and I can't be sure Eve isn't listening. It's not how I imagined it would be when we saw each other again. There seems to be an awkwardness between us, and I'm not sure why. Maybe it's because Jenny is worried about her mother, or maybe she's depressed about returning to Sutter's Bend. Whatever the reason, I get the feeling she doesn't want to talk.

Eve sleeps for most of the way, just waking up when we stop for gas and to stretch our legs.

It's late afternoon when we roll into Emmett Falls. With a long drive still ahead of us before we get to Sutter's Bend, I'd like to get back on the road as soon as possible, but Clara urges us to stay for dinner and Jenny wants to, so I don't insist. Letting her have this time with Clara is the least I can do for her.

"Now tell me about your trip to Eugene," Clara says when we are all seated around the table under the warm glow of the hanging lamp and Mrs. Duncan, a matronly woman in her fifties who has been her caretaker in Eve's absence, has deposited the last item, a plate of warm rolls, on the table.

My eyes meet Eve's across the table and she looks away. She seems subdued now, sullen even, compared to how animated she was before we went to Eugene. Maybe she's tired, or maybe she's disappointed her road trip is over.

I can't help noticing the contrast with Jenny, her face lit up and eyes shining as she describes the science building that she toured and its labs.

"I even found some job leads," Jenny says. "I think with more time I could find work. And a financial aid officer said they might be able to offer me more aid. Of course, it'll have to wait now until . . ." She falters, no doubt thinking of her mother. "But later . . ."

"That's wonderful news," Clara says. "How about you, Eve? Did you enjoy your time away?"

"I looked up a few old friends."

She shoots me a warning look. But I have no desire to contradict her. If she wants Clara to think she has friends in Eugene, that's her call. I reach for another roll and butter it. Soon Jenny and I will be on our way and Eve will be just a bad memory.

"I'm sorry about your mother," Clara tells Jenny. "I do hope everything works out."

"I do too," Jenny says. "I would never have left if I'd known."

"Don't blame your parents for keeping it secret. No doubt they were trying to spare you for as long as they could."

"I'm sure you're right, but I wish they had told me."

When dinner ends, Clara suggests a last look at the garden, and Jenny readily agrees. I suspect they want to talk privately one last time before we leave. Not eager to be left alone with Eve, I jump up and help Mrs. Duncan clear the table. Eve waits, watching me with narrowed eyes each time I return for more dishes. I give her a wide berth as long as I can, but when I reach for her water glass, she grabs my wrist, nearly making me spill it.

"Don't forget what I said," she hisses. "We're two of a kind, you and me. I know you in a way she never will."

I yank my hand away and make a dash for the kitchen. I don't tell Mrs. Duncan what just happened. Better to pretend it didn't. I don't want her to think there's something between Eve and me.

After that I hang out in the kitchen with Mrs. Duncan until Jenny is ready to leave. At least there, listening to Mrs. Duncan recount the misadventures of her nieces, nephews, and grandchildren, I'm fairly confident Eve will leave me in peace.

CHAPTER 16

Jenny

I know your mother is uppermost in your mind just now," Clara says. "But don't give up. Think of it as a setback. Life has many setbacks. You can't let them defeat you." Through the sliding glass doors of the sunroom, I can see the garden, lit by a few path lights under a low-hanging moon.

But it isn't what's waiting for me back in Sutter's Bend or the uncertainty of the future that I want to talk about in the short time we have left. It's something I've been turning over in my mind since my dinner with Malcolm.

"Can I ask you a question?"

"Of course. Ask away."

"I suppose this sounds a little odd, but do you think a woman scientist is better off pursuing her research on her own or collaborating with someone else?"

"That's an interesting question and a very difficult one to answer. In a way all great achievements are probably a result of collaborations or teamwork. We don't exist in a vacuum. We build on what others have discovered."

"I meant a partnership, like Pierre and Marie Curie."

"Ah, the Curies. A partnership and a marriage. I'm afraid I don't have an answer for you, Jenny. Choosing who to marry or whether to marry at all is just as problematic for a woman scientist as for any other woman who has a goal other than marriage. And I don't think that's changed a lot since I was young. But tell me, what prompted you to ask this?"

I hesitate, reluctant to tell her about Malcolm. After all, I barely know him. And considering how our dinner date ended, I may never see him again.

But now that I've asked her, maybe it's only fair that I explain myself, so I pluck up my nerve and launch in.

"While I was in Eugene, I met someone—a graduate student—who suggested we might work together on a project he's working on. He's using CRISPR on fruit flies."

"I see."

"But later he wants to do research on telomeres. If I help with the fruit fly project, I might get to work on the telomere project later."

"Fruit flies and telomeres. So what about you, Jenny? Are fruit flies and telomeres what you want to study?"

"I don't know."

"There are many choices out there. Don't be too quick to decide what you want to do with your life. A hasty choice may keep you from pursuing other research that may appeal to you more."

"But wouldn't it be a sort of ideal situation if we collaborated? I mean, he would *understand* . . ." I stop. Understand what? Understand what I was trying to do? Understand *me*?

To my relief Clara doesn't press me to explain. "Maybe he would and maybe he wouldn't. I could name a number of women scientists who did not get credit for the work they did because it went instead to a male colleague or husband. Just ask Einstein's wife. Or Lise Meitner, who had to flee Germany during World War II and let a male colleague take all the credit for discovering nuclear fission when the Nobel Award was handed out. Or Esther Lederberg, who had to watch her husband, her mentor, and a colleague—all men—receive a Nobel Prize for work to which she had contributed. It's a pretty dream to think that a marriage of minds will solve all problems, but it seldom works out like that. Such marriages are rare, and unfortunately some men prefer to keep the glory for themselves."

"Were you concerned about how much support you'd get from your husband when you married?"

"In the beginning, no, because I was young and I was in love. Later, yes, that was one of my concerns. I knew if Otto didn't support my research, something would suffer—either my research or our marriage. I tried my best to make both work, but eventually it was too much strain for our marriage and we divorced."

"So did you regret having married him?"

"No, never. Our marriage may not have worked out, but we had Rachel and we had twenty years together. Marriage grounded me in a way that my lab work didn't."

"Do you miss it—working in your lab?"

"I miss a lot of things, like losing my eyesight. There's a lot of letting go that comes with age. Now I concentrate on the small things—like growing roses in my garden."

I look at the garden beyond the sliding glass doors, steeped in shadows. "It's a beautiful garden."

"I can't see it with my eyes, but I see it in my mind. I have that and books and music."

I look out at the garden again, thinking how sad it is that she can't see it.

She reaches out and I take her hand. "You remind me of myself all those years ago. Before Rachel. Before Otto. Back when I was just starting out. I grew up on a farm in Minnesota. I was raised by my grandparents, who encouraged me to study hard and go to college. But they didn't understand why I wanted to study science. They thought I should be a teacher. To them that was the highest achievement they could conceive for me. To be a scientist—they couldn't imagine that. It was too removed from their experience. They thought I was aiming too high. Who did they know who was a scientist? No one. Oh, well, they tried the best they could. I'm grateful to them for all they did for me." She pats my hand. "It must be getting late. Are you sure you and Alec won't stay for the night?"

"He wants to get back, and I'm worried about my mother."

"I understand. I won't keep you, but I hope you'll write to me and let me know how things work out. And tell Alec to write to me too. He reminds me of someone I knew a long time ago."

I wait, hoping she'll tell me more, but she seems lost in thought.

"Shall I push you back?" I ask.

"No, I think I'll sit here for a little longer. Perhaps you could tell Mrs. Duncan I'm ready for my bath."

I say goodbye, kiss her cheek, and leave her there in the darkened room in her wheelchair, gazing blindly out at her garden and inward at old memories. My last view of her is her profile and the pale halo of her white hair.

At the front door Mrs. Duncan is talking to Alec while Eve stands nearby looking bored.

I join Eve. "Tired?"

"I suppose." She yawns.

"You were right when you advised me to go on to Eugene. I'm glad I did."

She leans closer and whispers in my ear. "I'm sorry."

I wonder if I misunderstood. "About what?" I look into her eyes. She might be a Nordic woman, pale, faintly freckled, the product of a land of ice and snow.

"I guess Alec didn't tell you."

"Tell me what?"

She smiles and gives a small shrug.

Alec throws me a desperate look. Mrs. Duncan is regaling him with a story about her grandchildren. I suppose it's time to rescue him, but before I can, Eve steps forward and flings an arm around his neck, pulls his head down, and kisses him on the mouth. There's a second of stunned silence in which Mrs. Duncan stops talking. Alec scowls as Eve steps back with a defiant toss of her head, not meeting anyone's eyes.

Alec looks at me. "Ready?" he asks as if nothing odd just happened.

I hurriedly tell Mrs. Duncan that Clara is ready for her bath.

There is a flurry of goodbyes as we leave. Outside a light rain is falling. We run to the car. Not until we are inside and belted up do I ask, "What was that about?"

Alec stares straight ahead through the windshield at the wet pavement gleaming under a streetlight. "Maybe you should ask Eve."

"Eve isn't here."

"No, thank god." He starts the engine. For a while neither of us says anything as we drive through the residential streets, the rain falling harder now. Once we reach the on-ramp to the highway, Alec breaks the silence.

"She tricked me into taking her to Eugene. She said she had friends there."

My first instinct is to defend Eve. He must be mistaken. Surely she didn't *trick* him. "Maybe she just wanted a break from taking care of Clara. You can't blame her for wanting to get away for a bit." I think of how badly I wanted to get away from Sutter's Bend.

"I wouldn't have minded if she'd just told me the truth."

I hear the hurt and anger in his voice and try again. "Maybe you should make allowances for her, given what she's been through."

He frowns. "You mean the car accident?"

"Car accident?"

"Yeah, how their car went off a bridge and all her family was killed."

"That's not . . . She told me her mother didn't want her. She left home. She didn't say anything about a car accident."

He glances at me. "She told me she was raised by her aunt after her family died in a car accident."

"I thought she said her mother remarried. She mentioned a stepsister. Are you sure you didn't misunderstand?"

"No, I didn't misunderstand."

I remember how helpful and friendly Eve was once she got over her initial aloofness and how she encouraged me to go to Eugene instead of back to Sutter's Bend. Why would she tell us different stories about her past?

"I'm sorry about your mother," Alec says. "I hated being the one to have to tell you."

His remark reminds me why I'm going home. My mother has cancer. It doesn't matter what Eve told him or told me.

"I should have known something was wrong. As far back as I can remember, my parents wanted me to go to college, and then for them to suddenly change . . . "

"They should have told you."

"I don't think I could bear it if anything happens to her."

My wild flight to Emmett Falls and then on to Eugene now seems selfish. My parents had so much to worry about, and I only added to it by running away. I could at least have checked my messages, but no, nothing seemed as important as putting as much distance as possible between me and Sutter's Bend. Anything else could wait, I told myself. Not in my wildest imaginings did it occur to me that my mother might be dying. What if Alec hadn't found me when he did? I might still be in Eugene, completely unaware of what was happening at home.

I glance at him, clenched jaw, eyes fixed on the road ahead, and my heart melts a little. I remember how determined I was just a few days ago to persuade him to go to college. Now it seems like a lifetime ago.

"I still think you should go to University of Oregon in the fall," I tell him.

"Who knows? Maybe I will."

"You changed your mind?"

"Maybe."

"What made you change your mind?"

He glances at me.

"Me?"

He smiles. "And my parents."

"I thought you were set against going into premed."

"I was. I still am."

"I don't understand."

"They're getting divorced."

How could I have forgotten that? He told me when he called me the night before I left home. Caught up in my own problems, I forgot about his.

"I'm sorry."

"Don't be. It's not your fault."

It's raining harder now. The windshield wipers sweep back and forth, and the highway rushes toward us in a swirl of droplets caught in the beams of our headlights. I wonder again why Eve kissed him just before we left. Is there something he isn't telling me? If I don't ask, I'm going to keep wondering.

"Did something happen between you and Eve?"

"No."

His face is stony. He grips the steering wheel as if his life depends on it. I hear again Eve's whisper in my ear. *I'm sorry.* Sorry for what? Why did she behave so differently tonight compared to several days ago? What changed? And why did she tell me one story about her family and Alec another? Whatever the explanation, clearly Alec doesn't want to talk about it. I tell myself to let it go.

"Clara wants you to write to her."

"Me?"

"Well, both of us."

"I can understand why she wants *you* to write to her, but why me?"

"You made an impression on her, I think."

He snorts. "Hasn't she ever met someone who has no clue what he wants to do with his life? I'm hardly unique."

"I think you are."

He glances at me, and his face softens. "I have no idea what you see in me. One day you're going to be a famous scientist, and I'll probably still be trying to figure out what I want to do when I grow up."

"Are you kidding? I'll be lucky if I'm not still working at the Golden Duck twenty years from now."

"No way." His voice is husky with tenderness. My most loyal defender. I feel a rush of affection for him.

"How come we didn't notice each other sooner?" I ask. "We were in dozens of classes together. We must have passed each other in the hall hundreds of times."

"Maybe when you see someone all the time, you don't really *see* them."

He might be right. It makes me wonder what else I've missed because I wasn't really looking. If it hadn't been for the party that night, I might never have noticed Alec.

"I'm sorry I ran off like that."

"It's okay. I get it. You felt like you had to go. And I didn't exactly help the situation when I showed up at your parents' restaurant that night."

"You were only trying to help."

"Yeah, by making everything worse."

I touch his arm. "No, please don't think that. What you did was brave."

"More like stupid."

"Maybe brave people do stupid things."

CHAPTER 17

Alec

Toby is sitting at the table eating a bowl of Cap'n Crunch when I walk into the kitchen the next morning. My mom is sipping a mug of coffee. She raises a single eyebrow when she sees me and scowls.

"Where have you been? No, wait. Don't tell me. I remember. You chased off after that girl."

I'm tempted to turn around and go back to bed. We got in late and I've only had a few hours of sleep. I'm not ready for my mother's sarcasm.

"Well, I hope she's worth it."

"She is." I open the fridge and survey my options. Frozen pancakes. Good enough. I shove a few into the microwave on a plate, hoping that, drowned in maple syrup, they won't taste like cardboard.

"Can I have pancakes too?" Toby asks, eyeing mine when they come out of the microwave.

"No, we don't have time," my mother says. "Now hurry up and finish. We have to leave in five minutes."

She's wearing a navy blue suit with a red neck scarf, so she must be on her way to her real estate office after dropping Toby at Summer Fun.

"By the way, Foley's called here yesterday wanting to know why you weren't at work," she says as I pour syrup over my pancakes.

"What did you tell them?"

"What could I tell them? I said you weren't here."

She could have said I was sick. But that's what I get for not calling them. Well, I'll think of some excuse to explain why I missed work for three days.

"Oh, and I need you to watch Toby tonight."

Watching Toby means I won't be able to see Jenny when she gets off work. It drives me nuts how my mother acts like I don't have a life of my own.

"Can't you get Mrs. Johnson to watch him?"

"It's not going to kill you to stay home a night and watch your brother."

"We can watch *It*," Toby says through a mouthful of Cap'n Crunch.

It's not as if we haven't already seen *It* more times than I can count.

"Toby, five minutes." She taps her watch with her finger and then walks out of the kitchen.

"So where's Mom off to tonight?" I ask Toby as I dig into my pancakes.

"She's got a date with Roger-Dodger." He casts an envious look at my pancakes.

A *date*? Seriously? Dad's only been gone a week.

"Who's Roger-Dodger?"

Toby shrugs. "Some guy."

That doesn't tell me much. Probably not worth it to quiz him further. I wonder if my dad knows my mom is seeing someone. Or cares. It's like my world is spiraling out of control. I wonder if Toby feels it too. If he does, he doesn't show it, and I'd be a jerk to point it out. He'll realize what's happening soon enough.

I push my plate toward him, half a pancake still on it. "Don't tell Mom."

He grins and stuffs the rest of the pancake into his mouth just as she shouts for him to hurry up.

I've barely gotten through the door at Foley's Hardware when Mrs. Crawford looks up while checking out a customer and spots me. I flash her a big smile. She's worked at Foley's for years, and I make a point of trying to stay on her good side. She doesn't smile back. Bad sign. "Frank wants to see you," she calls across the space between us. Frank is our manager. No doubt he wants to know why I wasn't at work this past weekend. Or wants to chew me out. Maybe both.

I'll tell the truth as nearly as I can since I can't claim to have been sick, thanks to my mom.

On my way to the back of the store, I run across Dustin restocking shelves in the plumbing aisle.

"Where were you, man?" he asks in a low voice.

"I had to go out of town."

"Frank was asking everybody if they knew where you were. He was really pissed."

This isn't reassuring. I keep walking until I reach the back of the store, where Frank has a cubicle. He's sitting there at his desk when I find him. He looks over the top of his glasses at me and scowls. I brace myself and prepare to explain how an emergency came up and I had to help a friend. I've hardly gotten started when he cuts me off. "I don't care if you had to help the Pope. You left us high and dry on a weekend. You're out of here, Morrissey."

I suspect arguing will just rile him more, and after all, he has a right to fire me if he wants, so I just nod and retreat. As I leave the store, I tell myself if I had to do it all over again, I'd still probably have gone in search of Jenny. Even if I'd called in sick, Frank might not have believed me. I regret losing my job, but there's not much I can do about it now.

Once I'm back in my car, I consider texting Jenny, but I don't want to tell her I lost my job. No reason to make her feel guilty. She has enough worries without me adding to them. And since I have nothing better to do, I might as well start looking for another job. Of course, in a backwater like Sutter's Bend, there aren't a lot of choices. For lack of a better idea, I head to the Shack to see if they're hiring. It's not the kind of job I'd prefer, but it would allow me to earn some cash until I leave for college in the fall, an option that's been looking more attractive ever since the threat of divorce turned my home life upside down. And it seems as good a time as any to text my father and let him know I'll attend University of Oregon in the fall if he's still willing to pay for it. I was hoping to talk to him about it in person, but who knows when he's coming home again. If ever.

At the Shack the manager looks me over skeptically and tells me to fill out an application on-line and send it in. He gives me no encouragement about my chances of being hired. I get the impression that it's a standard response to avoid the hassle of dealing with walk-ins like me. Better not hold my breath on that one.

After trying a few more places and getting similar reactions, I decide to take a break from my job search and stop by the Bookery. A little time in the labyrinth might be just what I need. It seems odd to walk into the bookstore at an hour when normally I'd be at work, sort of like playing hooky from school. It's mid-afternoon and business is slow, but that's fine with me. I'd just as soon have the place to myself. Mrs. Kilmer is behind the counter, a middle-aged woman who can skewer you with a look over her bifocals. I ignore her and head straight for the horror section deep in the labyrinth. Before long I find an old Stephen King novel I haven't read. While I should conserve my cash now that I have no job, I can't resist the urge to buy it. Anyway, it's a used book and doesn't cost much.

While Mrs. Kilmer rings me up, I notice a small help wanted sign on the counter.

"How do I apply?" I ask, pointing at the sign.

She looks at me and sighs. Then she slaps an application down on the counter. I fill it out because what do I have to lose? Besides, if I don't, someone else may snap up the job first. I push the finished application back to her, then wander over to the new books section to postpone for a few more minutes returning to my job search.

"Hey, kid, are you the one interested in the job?" asks an older man in glasses as I'm about to walk out the door. I don't particularly appreciate being called a kid, but since I want the job I don't object. I've seen him around before. His name, according to his name tag, is Dave, and it turns out he's the manager.

He invites me into an office the size of a broom closet and glances over my application. Then he asks when I can start, tells me the pay—less than I was making at Foley's, but I'm desperate—and hesitates when I tell him I'm headed for college in the fall. He tells me one of his employees just quit and he's short-handed. After a few seconds of deliberation, he decides to give me the job but warns me that the first time I show up late or miss work, he'll fire me.

I go home feeling like things are looking up. Not until I walk in the house do I remember I have to babysit Toby, but even that doesn't dampen my spirits.

I find Toby in the kitchen, unsupervised, eating pizza from a cardboard box. Ordinarily Mom wouldn't let him have pizza for dinner, but it seems like rules have suddenly loosened up.

"That's your half," he says, pointing at the half he has separated from the other remaining pieces, presumably his. All the green peppers have been heaped on my half since Toby doesn't like green peppers.

Pizza's fine with me, but first I want a word with Mom before she leaves. Toby tells me she's upstairs getting ready for her date with Roger-Dodger.

I find her in the bathroom, the door standing open while she puts on lipstick in front of the mirror. She's wearing her little black dress, heels, and a pair of earrings Dad gave her for their anniversary. I catch a whiff of perfume. Whoever this guy is, she's going all out for him.

"So who is this Roger?" I ask, lounging in the doorway.

"Just someone I know," she says, blotting her lips with a tissue.

"You're going on a *date*?"

"I'm going out to dinner with a friend."

"You look like you're going on a date."

She throws me an exasperated look. "Well, what does it matter if I am? If your father's dating, I don't see why I can't too."

Because you're still married, I want to shout, but I don't because she has a point. In a way this is Dad's fault. And he's still married too.

"What time will you be home?" I ask instead.

She smiles. "That's a switch—you asking me what time *I'll* be home."

"I need to know."

"Why? What does it matter?"

"I told Jenny I'd see her after she gets off work."

"Honestly, Alec, you can go one night without running over there to see her. I doubt her parents appreciate it, especially given what her mother's going through."

"Will you be out later than nine?"

"I don't know. And don't you run off and leave your brother alone."

The doorbell rings, and our heads swivel toward the stairs.

"That's probably him. How do I look?" She turns around.

"Terrific," I say sourly.

Then I make a dash for the stairs, taking them two at a time because I want to check out this Roger-Dodger before he whisks my mother away.

When I throw open the door, I find myself face-to-face with a man with a comb-over dressed in a sports jacket that hangs loosely. And wing tips. No one wears wing tips anymore. He breaks into a smile that looks like he just had his teeth whitened for a toothpaste commercial.

"You must be Roger."

"And you must be Alec." He thrusts out a pudgy hand, and I have no choice but to shake it.

While he goes on beaming at me, Mom comes tripping down the stairs in her heels and nudges me aside.

"I see you've met Alec."

"Wow. Look at you." He looks her up and down and whistles.

It nearly makes me gag. Why would she go out with this clown? Maybe he's a client after all, and she's trying to sell him an overpriced property. But no, she wouldn't be wearing her little black dress and the earrings Dad gave her if he were just a client. At least I don't think she would.

I watch them walk to his white Honda Civic, his hand on the small of her back. She laughs at something he said. I stifle the urge to yell at him to get his hands off my mom.

Feeling thoroughly out of sorts, I slam the door and head for the kitchen to see if Toby has left me any pizza.

"Did you meet Roger-Dodger?" he asks, licking his fingers.

"Yeah, he's an asshole. Don't tell Mom I said that."

"Okay. I wish Dad would come home."

"That makes two of us."

Staring at the remaining slices of pizza, I realize I didn't tell Mom about my new job. I haven't told Jenny either. Pulling out my phone, I find a text from Dad, a reply to the one I sent him earlier. He says he'll pay for University of Oregon if I go into premed, just as we agreed. So it looks like I go into premed or I stay right here in Sutter's Bend and watch my mom go out with men like Roger-Dodger. Great.

CHAPTER 18

Jenny

Gone for four days and nothing's changed. I'm back at the Golden Duck, rushing between tables, delivering plates of orange chicken and sweet and sour pork to customers who wonder why their food can't be served faster. It's as if I never left. I thought I could leave all of this behind, but I was wrong. Did I really think I could escape Sutter's Bend so easily?

"Hey, snap out of it!" Becca says as she hurries past with four bowls of egg flower soup on a tray. "Get table four before *she* does." Her eyes pivot toward our new server, dressed in a skirt too short which shows off her long legs, her blonde ponytail bobbing over the heads of her customers.

I sigh. Yes, there is one change. The new hire. April Evans. I understand that my departure left the Duck short-handed, but April Evans? What possessed my parents to hire *her*? And even more puzzling, what possessed her to take a job waiting tables at the Duck? She looks as if she belongs in a very different setting—the Shack maybe. She has barely spoken to me since my shift started. Of course, I've barely spoken to her. I wonder if they'll let her go now that I'm back? After all, if my parents are short on money, how can they afford another waitress? Then again maybe they're worried I won't stay. They really don't need to worry. I'm not going to bail when Mom needs me here.

Later when the dinner crowd thins out, I find a moment alone with Becca while she's clearing a table.

"Whose idea was it to hire her?" I ask.

"Oh, that would be Glen."

I glance back at the kitchen, where his head is bent over whatever he's cooking. Why would he have recommended April? There are many other girls who would be better suited to the Golden Duck. What does April know about Chinese cuisine or working in a Chinese restaurant?

"Why would Glen recommend her? I don't get it."

Becca gives me a look like I'm dense.

Surely not. I glance back at the kitchen again. Glen and April? But they have nothing in common. They're total opposites. Becca must be wrong. But now she's got me curious, so I find an excuse to slip into the kitchen, where Glen is alone, my father having left a little earlier to go home and check on my mom.

"Busy night," Glen says, glancing up.

I get straight to the point. "I hear you recommended April."

He shrugs. "We needed the help."

"Are you guys dating?"

"What? God, no." He looks flustered. "It's not like that."

"Then why?"

"She needed a job. And we needed someone to take up the slack with you gone and your mom sick."

Me gone and my mom sick. The words careen about in my brain like balls in a pinball machine. A wave of guilt sweeps over me. How could I have let everybody down so badly?

"Besides, my mom and dad would have a fit." He avoids my eyes.

So he *is* interested in April. Poor Glen. There's no way he has a chance with her. Girls like that don't know guys like Glen exist.

Before I can say another word, April sweeps into the kitchen, tugging off her apron. For a split second I think she's quitting, but no, she's just done for the night.

She glances at me. "Tell your dad I needed to leave early. No problem, right?"

"No, it's okay. I'll tell him."

"See ya, Glen," she says over her shoulder as she heads for the door.

He watches her every step of the way, his face a mixture of yearning and hopelessness.

"You should ask her out," I tell him when she's gone.

"No way. She'd never go out with me. I think she's dating Tristan Barnett."

Our star football player. That sounds about right.

"You should ask her anyway. What's the worst that could happen? She might say no."

"I told you, my parents would have a fit."

Glen's parents are good friends of my parents and have always treated me as if I were one of the family. No doubt, like my parents, they thought one day I'd be a part of their family.

"How are they taking our breakup?"

"I haven't told them."

"You've got to tell them."

"I know, but I'm waiting for the right time."

I watch him chopping scallions, ginger, and garlic. "Do you want me to tell them?"

"No."

"I think you should ask April out."

"What if she thinks I'm harassing her and complains—or quits?"

I shrug. "We'll get another girl. And anyway I'm back now."

"But for how long?"

Another wave of guilt washes over me. Does everybody have to keep reminding me? Okay, I wasn't here when my parents needed me, but I'm here now. I'll make it up to them.

"I can't go off anywhere while my mom's sick."

"I'm sorry about your mom."

I nod, not trusting myself to speak.

"And I'm sorry your college plans fell through. I know how much you were looking forward to going. You still seeing Alec?"

"Yes."

"Your parents okay with that?"

"I think so. Maybe they're too worried about Mom to worry about me for now."

Becca rushes up to the counter and glares at me. "How about some help out here?"

I dash out to help her, feeling guilty again.

CHAPTER 19

Alec

I figure my new job will be easy compared to Foley's. I might even have time to sit around and read when we aren't busy. But almost as soon as I walk in the door, Dave puts me to work restocking shelves. Every time I emerge from the labyrinth, Mrs. Kilmer fixes me with that beady-eyed stare of hers, as if she's just waiting for me to screw up. I have no idea why she has taken such a dislike to me, but since I can't afford to lose the job, I try to be extra polite to her. For a while I have to stand beside her while she explains how to handle sales, which I have to know so I can help out when things get busy or if she's out sick. I quickly get the impression she thinks I'm not too bright.

It turns out I'm not the only grunt worker in the store. There's also Liv, who was hired earlier in the summer. She's one year behind me in school, probably the only girl in her class still wearing pigtails. But she's a human calculator, and she knows where every book in the store is without checking the inventory. I can't say the same about myself.

"Don't let her get to you," Liv tells me. "She's kind of a prima donna."

"How so?"

"Just wait. You'll see."

I don't have long to wait.

About mid-morning mothers begin to arrive with their little kids in tow and head for the Children's Corner, where Liv and I have set up folding chairs. They all seem to know each other, and with their arrival, the bookstore springs to life.

Mrs. Kilmer turns cashier duties over to Dave and goes to greet the mothers, transforming in the blink of an eye from the Wicked Witch of the West into Mary Poppins—without the umbrella.

"You should watch this," Dave tells me, so I join Liv where she's lurking behind the circle of mothers.

Mrs. Kilmer seats herself in a chair facing the semi-circle of expectant mothers and children like a queen on her throne surrounded by adoring attendants. She beams at them and holds up a book.

"Who knows what this is?" she asks.

"Curious George," chime a chorus of small voices.

She nods approvingly and, opening the book, begins to read, slowly and looking around at them, her voice rising and then sinking to a whisper, her arm flung out dramatically. The children watch her, enthralled.

Liv nudges me with her elbow. "She's good, isn't she?"

"I guess so," I admit grudgingly, although how hard can it be to impress a bunch of little kids?

* * *

At the end of the day I pick up Jenny after she gets off work and we go to the rocks. We couldn't go there the night before because my mom didn't get in until midnight. By then it was too late. And we couldn't meet at the rocks in the morning because Jenny wanted to be at the hospital when her mother got chemo. But finally on our second night back we manage to spend some time together at the rocks.

As we watch the breakers roll in by the light of the moon, she tells me about her day, and I tell her about mine. For a while all that matters is we're together.

"Have you heard anything from your dad?" she asks after we've shared the day's high points and low points.

"No, just that text I told you about."

"So what will you do?"

"I don't know."

She leans back in my arms and sighs. I feel the warmth of her body against mine. Below us the waves crash against the rocks. I kiss the top of her head and breathe in the honeysuckle scent of her shampoo. The breeze blowing in from the ocean has a chill in it and smells of saltwater. I know we can't stay long, and I want to savor every moment of our time together while I can.

"I don't suppose you could *pretend* to go into premed?" she asks.

"At what point would I tell my dad? Besides, I'm not sure I want to be at University of Oregon if you're not there too."

"You can't stay in Sutter's Bend just because of me."

"Why not?"

"You have to think about your future."

I have, and I can't imagine a future without Jenny in it. "Tyler said maybe I can get a job at his father's sawmill. I'd make more than I do at the Bookery."

"But is that really what you want to do?"

"Well, not forever."

"Don't you see you have to go to University of Oregon? I don't want you to stay here because of me. I'd feel so guilty."

"But I don't want to go into premed, and I can't take my dad's money and *not* go into premed. It wouldn't be right."

"What's your mom say?"

"I haven't asked her. She's all caught up in her job and she's going out with this Roger-Dodger."

"Roger-Dodger?"

"That's what Toby calls him."

"I take it you don't like him."

"I don't see what she sees in him."

"You think that's what we'll be like someday—like our parents?"

"God, I hope not."

"Me too. I want to do something with my life. I want my life to mean something. Is that so much to ask?"

"Of course not."

"You must think I'm crazy."

"No, that's one of the things I love about you. You know what you want to do. I wish I did."

"Do you really think we'll get out of here someday?"

"Absolutely."

"What would I do without you?"

She tilts her head up, our lips meet, and what had seemed perfect a moment before, now seems even more perfect.

CHAPTER 20

Jenny

I've settled into my old routine—although now it includes accompanying my mother to her chemo treatments and staying by her side when she gets sick afterward. I see Alec as often as I can. Sometimes we meet after I jog in the morning and other times after I get off work at night.

With each passing day Emmett Falls and the University of Oregon seem farther away and less real. I tried to write to Clara but ended up tearing up the letter. It's just too hard to write about my mother. I tell myself she'll be okay—the doctors will save her—but secretly I fear they won't. It's almost as if I'm being punished for wanting to leave, and so I try not to think about what will come next and live day by day, telling myself I'll make whatever sacrifices I must, just so long as she gets to live.

And then one night Malcolm walks into the Golden Duck. Tall, lanky, pushing his glasses up with one finger and glancing around as if he's not quite sure he's in the right place. Becca is on door duty. He bends his head and says something to her. He must have asked her about me, because she turns and looks at me, eyes wide. I've just stepped out of the kitchen with a plate of chicken wings and a bowl of beef chow mein. I stare at him, trying to process the fact that he's standing there beside Becca. What's he doing here?

His eyes meet mine and he grins. It's too late to pretend I didn't see him. I force myself to smile. Becca signals to me, and so reluctantly I thread my way between the tables and join them.

"Malcolm," I say, "this is a surprise."

Becca stands rooted to the spot, no doubt dying to know who he is. I thrust the tray I'm holding at her and pluck the menu she's holding from her hand.

"I had to come see the Golden Duck after all you told me about it," Malcolm says, looking about the room, now more than half full.

I don't remember telling him anything about the Duck except maybe that I wasn't happy working here. It wasn't an invitation for him to visit. But now he's here, and I have to make him feel welcome. After all, he's a customer.

I show him to a table and hand him the menu.

"Could you join me?" he asks, glancing about at the other diners and no doubt noticing he's the only one seated alone.

We're busy and I should be helping, but it seems rude to leave him sitting by himself. Besides, if I do, he'll probably be watching my every move—an unnerving prospect. Why did he have to come? It's not as if I encouraged him. Or at least I didn't mean to. People are starting to stare. I sink onto a chair across from him to be less conspicuous.

"So what do you recommend?" he asks, looking over the menu.

"The Peking duck." It's what we always recommend when customers ask. My father is particularly proud of his Peking duck.

"How about for you?"

"I've already eaten. Besides, I'm working."

He smiles nervously. "You're probably wondering why I'm here."

"I assume you weren't just passing through Sutter's Bend."

"It *is* sort of off the beaten track."

"So why are you here?"

"I've been thinking about you. I'm afraid I didn't express myself as well as I might have the last time I saw you. I didn't realize you would just disappear like that. I hope it wasn't because of me."

"It wasn't."

"I suppose it was because of your mother then?" He sees my look of surprise. "Your brother told me."

"You talked to my brother?"

"Yes . . . and his roommate."

"How did you know where he lives?

"His name was on his mailbox. There weren't any other Chens."

He actually tracked down Paul at Aldergate Terrace to find me? I can just imagine what Paul will have to say about that.

He reaches across the table and grabs my hand. "Look, I want you to know I meant it when I said we would make a great team. My offer still stands. About the fruit fly project, I mean."

I would pull my hand away, but I don't want to make a scene.

"You don't understand. I can't enroll in the fall. I have to stay here in Sutter's Bend."

"Why?"

"My parents don't have the money. My mom's cancer bills."

"Oh." His eyes fall to the menu, but he's not really looking at it.

"I'm sorry you came all this way."

"Maybe I could talk to the head of my department and see if they could swing a scholarship for you."

A second scholarship? Is that really a possibility? Could I go after all? I feel the old surge of hope, but then I quash it. My mother needs me here in Sutter's Bend. Besides, after talking to Clara, I have doubts about teaming up with Malcolm. As she said, I should be careful about choosing too hastily what I want to research. When I first met Malcolm, I was flattered he noticed me and wanted to work with me, but now I see a relationship with him would likely not be one of equals. I suspect it would be about what *he* wanted. I can see what the future might look like with him, and I don't think it's what I want. Of course, I can't tell him that. He would be offended or he would argue. With other diners watching us, I don't want to have an argument. But I have to tell him something. I pull my hand away.

"I have a boyfriend. I should have told you."

He looks startled. "You do?"

"Yes, I'm sorry I forgot to mention that. Do you still want the duck?"

His finger taps the menu as he thinks about it. "Actually, I think I'll pass on the duck. I'm not as hungry as I thought I was."

Our chairs scrape on the tile floor as we stand.

"If you change your mind about that scholarship . . . ," he says.

"I don't think I will."

He nods and glances around the restaurant again. "It's a nice little business your folks have here."

"Thanks."

"Maybe it's better this way."

I'm not sure what he means. That I'm too young? Too naïve? Not right for his project? I don't ask. Maybe he's trying to hurt me a little because I hurt his pride.

I watch him walk out the door without looking back.

Becca sidles up. "So what was that all about?"

"Just someone I met at Eugene."

"You never mentioned you met somebody."

"Don't you dare tell Mom and Dad."

"Isn't he a little old for you? Is he a professor?"

"No, and just forget you ever saw him."

"What did he want?"

"Apparently not the Peking duck."

"Who was that guy who came in tonight?" Glen asks casually as he drives Becca and me home after work. I suspect he was just waiting to ask.

I resist looking at Becca in the backseat. I have a feeling she isn't plugged into her phone for once. She's probably all ears to hear my answer.

I strive to sound matter-of-fact. "He's a grad student at the University of Oregon. He wanted to know if I'd be interested in joining a research project he's working on."

"I thought you weren't going to University of Oregon in the fall."

"I'm not."

He's quiet for a bit. Then he smiles. "So Alec has some competition?"

"Look, can you just keep this between us? I don't want to upset my parents. If it gets back to them . . ."

"Sure," Glen says. "I'll keep your secret, but what about everyone else who was there tonight? Becca and April and I weren't the only ones who saw . . . your friend from out of town."

My friend from out of town. I don't like the sound of that. I can just imagine how it could spread in Sutter's Bend.

And he's right. Any number of people—some of whom know my parents—saw me sit down at a table for two with Malcolm and let him hold my hand. You can bet it won't be long before my parents hear. I'd better tell them before they hear it from someone else.

So I walk into the house determined to tell my parents about Malcolm's visit to the Duck. They're in the living room, Mom lying on the sofa, Dad sitting beside her holding her hand, the volume on the TV turned so low they can't possibly be listening to it.

"How'd it go?" my father asks, looking up. "Any problems?"

"No, no problems," I say quickly, glancing at Becca. She rolls her eyes and leaves, to my relief. It's going to be hard enough to tell them about Malcom without her standing there listening to every word. "But there was this guy who came in. Someone I met in Eugene. A grad student." I have their full attention. They wait for me to continue. "He came to ask me if I'd join his research project on gene-editing, but I told him I couldn't because I won't be going to University of Oregon in the fall."

My father frowns. "Someone drove all the way from Eugene to ask you to join a research project? Was there no one else he could ask?"

"I'm sure he'll find someone," I say hurriedly. "There are plenty who would jump at the opportunity."

"I'm so sorry," my mother says. "I know how much you were looking forward to starting college in the fall."

The dark circles under her eyes make my heart ache. I didn't mean to make her feel guilty. "No, it's okay. I just wanted you to know about this guy who came to the Duck tonight in case someone else tells you he was there." I'm not doing a good job of explaining. Instead of making Malcolm's visit sound innocent, I'm making it seem suspicious.

"How well do you know this grad student?" my father asks.

I feel my spine straighten. I want to tell him that I'm not a child anymore. I may not know Malcolm well, but I'm perfectly capable of making my own decisions.

"I might take him up on his offer if I were going to University of Oregon in the fall, but since I'm not, what does it matter?"

Then, before they can ask more questions, I excuse myself and leave the room. At least now they won't be surprised if someone tells them about Malcolm coming to the Duck.

CHAPTER 21

Alec

I nearly got fired today. Dave caught me reading in the labyrinth. I thought nobody would notice, and I got distracted when I found a used copy of *The Shining* wedged behind some other old paperbacks on a bottom shelf in the horror section. I was only going to read for five minutes, but I lost track of time. Dave really bawled me out. If I want to keep my job, I'll have to be more careful in the future.

When I get home, Mom's getting ready to go out again. She's been out with Roger-Dodger nearly every night this week. I've tried to tell her he's a loser, but it makes no difference. She doesn't care what I think.

There's no dinner waiting, but at least Toby's already eaten, so I heat up a frozen dinner in the microwave. The timer dings as Mom breezes into the kitchen wearing a red dress I haven't seen before.

"New dress?" I ask.

"As a matter of fact, yes. I'm surprised you noticed."

I smell perfume as she brushes past me on her way to the sink. New dress *and* perfume? And all this effort is for old Roger-Dodger?

"Did your day go okay, sweetie?" she asks after she fills a small glass with water and takes a sip.

"Great," I say without enthusiasm. I could tell her I almost got fired for reading on the job, but I know what she'd say—it's time I got serious and grew up.

"I heard you and Jenny broke up," she says. "I don't want you to take it too hard. She really wasn't right for you. I'm sure you'll find somebody else in no time."

"We didn't break up."

"You didn't?"

"I think I'd know."

"I heard she broke up with you. Something about dating one of her professors. Carol at the office told me."

"Why is Carol at the office an expert on *my* dating life?"

"So you didn't break up?"

"No, we didn't."

The doorbell rings.

"Mom!" Toby yells.

"That's probably Roger," she says. "Now make sure Toby's in bed by nine."

I don't bother to answer, and she doesn't bother to wait for an answer. I take my nuked Salisbury steak out of the microwave. Why would some woman at her office have told her Jenny and I broke up? Since when are we the subject of water cooler gossip at Mom's realty office?

I check my phone to see if I have any texts from Jenny—just in case. I don't, but there is one from Dustin. He wants to know if it's true that Jenny and I broke up. I stare at the message, shocked that he has somehow heard the same rumor as my mom.

Of course, it isn't true, but still it worries me. I could call Jenny and ask her if she's heard the rumor, but if she goes all silent and I can't see her face, I'll suspect the worst. I know it can't be true, and yet the rumor came from somewhere. It's the possibility that it *could* be true which bothers me. Jenny is really smart. Why wouldn't a professor be attracted to her? And if she can get a professor, why date me? Not only am I not a science geek, I have no idea what I want to do. Maybe while she's stuck here in Sutter's Bend, she'll be satisfied to hang out with me, but what about when she leaves? What hope do I have then?

There's only one way to find out if there's any truth to the rumor. I have to look into her eyes when I ask her.

So the next morning I park along the route Jenny takes when she jogs and wait for her to show up.

I'm leaning against my Camaro, reading a paperback, when she jogs into sight. She sees me and comes over to lean against the Camaro with me. It's still early with a breeze blowing from the ocean. She's wearing shorts and a T-shirt, her hair pulled back in a ponytail, and she's a little out of breath and perspiring. With her standing next to me, my qualms fall away. I can tell by her smile and the way her eyes light up when she looks at me that nothing has changed between us.

"What are you reading?" she asks, nodding at my book.

I show her the cover. Black with bold white print. *World War Z.*

She rolls her eyes. "You're incorrigible."

"How's your mom today?"

"So far it's a good day."

Suddenly I don't want to talk about the rumor. And that's probably all it is. Just a rumor. I should forget about it. Jenny's standing in front of me, very real, very much alive, and there's no indication she wants to break up. If I tell her about the rumor, she'll probably laugh.

"What's up?" she asks.

"Did you know there's a rumor going around that we broke up?"

"What? Well, that's news to me."

I feel reassured. The rumor was somebody's idea of a bad joke. I was silly to give it a second's thought.

"I heard you're dating a professor."

"*What?*" Now she sounds alarmed. "Who said that?"

I'm surprised by her reaction. "Well, first my mother. And then Dustin."

"Your *mother?*"

She knows my mother doesn't approve of her. I shouldn't have mentioned my mother. "Don't worry about it. It was just a stupid rumor."

"It's my fault." She looks down at her sneakers.

"What do you mean?"

"There was this grad student I met when I was in Eugene—Malcolm Whitmore."

My heart stops. All my fears come rushing back.

"He came to the Duck Sunday night to ask if I'd join this team he's put together. He's doing a gene-editing study with fruit flies. I told him no. I mean, I can't since I'm not going to University of Oregon in the fall. And even if I were, I'm not sure I'd want to."

My mind struggles to grasp what she's saying. She met someone when she was in Eugene? A grad student? And he turned up at the Duck looking for her? I really doubt that it was just to ask her to join the team he's put together.

And she had lots of time to tell me about him on the long ride home from Eugene and said nothing.

"Why didn't you tell me?"

"I didn't think it was important."

Not important? She was offered a chance to work on a science project with a graduate student. Knowing Jenny, that must have been quite a temptation. I'm surprised she turned it down.

"I'm sorry. I should have told you."

"He came a long way to talk to you."

"I didn't ask him to come. Anyway, it doesn't matter since I have to stay here."

"If you were going to start at University of Oregon in the fall, would you have said yes?"

"I don't know. I might have."

I look at her standing there in the sunlight. Maybe this time I get a reprieve, but what about next time? Sooner or later she'll notice I don't have anything to offer her. I push that thought aside. After all, she did tell him no.

"Meet me at the rocks after work?" I ask.

"I'm not sure. I may have to work late. I'll let you know."

She puts her arms around my neck, and I pull her close while we kiss. If anybody's watching, I don't care. Let Sutter's Bend gossip all it wants.

"I'll text you," she says before she jogs off again.

I watch until she's out of sight, wishing we at least had a meeting at the rocks tonight to look forward to.

Dave is at the counter setting up the cash drawer when I walk into the Bookery. Liv is restocking shelves She waves and bends over her carton of books.

"Where's Mrs. Kilmer?" I ask, surprised not to see the dragon lady behind the counter.

"She called in sick," Dave says.

Usually this would be enough to brighten my day, but today is different. I'm wondering if I should just give up and tell my dad I'm ready to go into premed. I could stop trying to figure out what I want to do and accept my fate. It would allow me to leave Sutter's Bend. No more having to watch my mom go out with Roger-Dodger. No more having to babysit Toby at night. But it would also mean no more Jenny.

"Why the long face?" Liv says when I join her and grab several books from her carton to put on the shelves.

"You ever think about the future?" I ask her.

She shrugs. "Of course. Doesn't everybody?"

"So what do you want to do? Is this what you see yourself doing ten years from now?" I glance at the books surrounding us.

"Don't be crazy. This is summer work. I'm saving for college, same as you."

Same as me. She's right. I shouldn't lose sight of what I want. Or what I *don't* want. What I don't want is to study premed. And while it's tempting to let my father pay for my college education, I can't take his money if I have to study to be a doctor to get it. Or even pretend to. It just wouldn't be honest. I'd hate myself.

"Better get the Children's Corner set up," Dave calls from behind the counter. "The mothers will soon be here."

Liv and I exchange glances. I assume Dave will read to them since Mrs. Kilmer isn't here. This should be interesting. I wonder what kind of reader Dave is. I've never seen him get excited about anything, unless you count when he caught me reading in the labyrinth yesterday. Somehow I can't picture him doing the Children's Hour.

Fifteen minutes later the chairs are set up and everything's ready as the mothers start to arrive, carrying their children, holding them by the hand, or letting them run free. Soon it's noisy and chaotic as the bookstore transforms into a preschool.

"So who's going to read?" I ask Dave.

"You are," he says, looking at me with an amused expression.

"Me?" I hope he's not serious.

"Better get ready. Grab a book. Doesn't matter which one. You're on in a couple of minutes. Don't keep them waiting."

"But I don't know how to do this."

"Nothing to it."

I think he's enjoying putting me on the spot. Maybe it's his way of getting back at me for slacking off yesterday.

"Don't worry," Liv tells me. "You've got this."

"Easy for you to say," I mutter.

Why couldn't he have asked her to do it?

"Look, how about this one?" She holds up *The Wonky Donkey*.

I shake my head. Then I see a book I used to read to Toby when he was little—*Where the Wild Things Are*.

Liv looks dubious, but I'm running out of time. I head to the reader's chair with the book and look around the circle of expectant faces. The mothers start shushing their children. Everyone's watching me, waiting for me to start. Even the little kids stare at me like they're expecting something I probably can't deliver. I wish I could make a break for the door. My heart must be thumping so loud they can all hear it. *Read it like you did with Toby*, I tell myself. And so I start. I jump out of my chair and start stomping about. The kids squeal and scatter. I hold up the book to show the first picture. A few of the kids start to follow me, and soon we're all pretending to be monsters. The monsters get bigger and scarier as I turn the pages. The kids watch me with big eyes, wondering what will come next. I notice Liv standing by a bookcase, a hand over her mouth to keep from laughing. I climb on the chair and then jump off it and several kids scream. One little one starts to cry. I wonder if Dave will fire me for frightening the kids. I lead my followers around the circle again. There are more of them this time, including a toddler who keeps falling down. And then we do the monster march, shoulders hunched, arms hanging down, faces grimacing. Some mothers cheer, a few look horrified.

When it's over, Liv gives me a thumbs up. Dave stands beside her looking impassive. When does he not look impassive? I pick my way through the mothers and children, trying not to step on anyone.

"Was that okay?" I ask Dave.

He shrugs. "Not bad for a first time."

"Don't pay any attention to him," Liv says. "They loved it."

I feel as if I just ran a marathon, one I thought I couldn't run. I have to admit it was pretty cool to see the kids' eyes grow big. I wonder if Dave will let me do it again sometime.

I'm still feeling good when I get off work in the early evening. I wonder if Mom's going out with Roger-Dodger tonight, but not even the thought of her and the awful Roger is enough to dampen my spirits.

I pull into the driveway behind a black BMW. One of Mom's friends? No blare of TV greets me when I step into the house a minute later, just low voices in the living room. A lamp throws a muted light on my mother and her guest. As I draw nearer, I recognize with a shock that long white-blonde braid and the curve of her neck even before she turns her head.

CHAPTER 22

Jenny

It's a busy evening at the Duck. I'm working in the kitchen so my dad can stay home with my mom. I'm not the cook he is, but I can manage. Both Becca and I have been trained to take over when the need arises. It seems odd that neither my mom nor my dad is here, but then these days nothing seems quite normal.

Glen glances over at me. "You okay?"

He's asked me that a dozen times already. I stand a little straighter to show him that I am.

"I could make Peking duck blindfolded," I assure him.

He grins. "Me too."

I wonder what we'll do in the fall when he leaves for college. My dad and I can probably handle the kitchen, but April will be gone too, and if Mom is still sick, we'll be short-handed. Even more so if one of us has to stay with her, as my dad did tonight. We'll need to hire more help.

April walks up to the counter and tells Glen she needs two orders of shrimp.

"Have you asked her out yet?" I ask when she's out of earshot.

"I'm working on it."

Which means he hasn't.

Becca charges up to the counter. "The woman at table six wants to talk to the manager. What do we do?"

I look across the room. My least favorite customer, the woman with the pencil-thin eyebrows and red lips, is sitting at table six with her husband and another couple.

"Guess I'd better get this," Glen says, starting to remove his plastic gloves.

"No, I'll get it."

"Are you sure?"

I nod and peel off my own gloves. Then I take a deep breath before stepping into the dining room. *Just don't let her get under your skin*, I tell myself.

As I approach, the two couples are talking genially enough. I stop beside the lady with the red lips, assuming she's the one with a complaint.

"Is there a problem?" I ask politely.

She looks me up and down, frowning. "I asked for the manager. You aren't the manager."

The other woman titters, and the men look embarrassed.

"My father isn't here at the moment," I tell her. "Is there something I can help you with?"

"Why isn't he here? If he's the manager, he should be here."

"He had a family matter to attend to." I wonder if she knows about my mother's cancer. Maybe it doesn't make any difference to her. She's not exactly the compassionate sort.

"Well, there must be someone else in charge."

"That would be me."

"Very well. This shrimp chow mein is a disgrace. Whoever is responsible for cooking it should be fired."

I remind myself not to let her upset me. You must always be polite to the customer. That has been drilled into me since I was old enough to work at the Duck. "Would you like to order something else?" I ask.

"No, I would not. I ordered the shrimp chow mein and that's what I want. Just not this dreadful stuff that you are passing off as shrimp chow mein."

"Would you like me to take it away?"

"No, I want to talk to the manager."

"As I just explained, he isn't available."

By now people at the nearest tables have stopped talking and are watching us.

"Do you know who I am?" she demands.

"Mrs. Pang."

She seems slightly mollified that I know, but it doesn't stop her. "Do you know who my husband is?"

Her husband keeps his eyes on the plate of Peking Duck in front of him. He's a partner at Dawes and Pang, a local law firm, but I'm not going to give her the satisfaction of saying that.

"Do you want me to take it away?" I repeat.

"And then what am I supposed to eat for dinner?"

The entire restaurant has gone silent, waiting to hear what I'll say.

"I have no idea."

I reach for the plate of shrimp chow mein and she grabs my arm. The shrimp chow mein spills into her lap before I can stop it.

"You stupid, clumsy girl! Look what you've done."

"I'm sorry." I stare in disbelief at the shrimp chow mein in her lap.

"You did that on purpose."

Before I can think what to do, Glen and Becca are beside me. He has a pan and a mop. She has wet cloths. Then April is there too, tugging my arm, pulling me away. "We'll get this," she says as she walks me toward the kitchen.

"My dress!" the woman wails behind me. "She's ruined it."

Once in the kitchen, I retreat to the only place where I can hide, the employee restroom. I sink to the floor, bury my face in my hands, and burst into tears. I think about what my dad will say when he hears. He trusted me to keep everything operating smoothly, and I've botched it. I'm not cut out for this work. I'm hopelessly incompetent. There's no way I can do this for the rest of my life.

A tap on the door.

"Who is it?"

"It's me."

I crack the door open and see Becca, looking worried.

"You okay?"

"Dad's going to kill me."

"No, he's not. It was an accident."

April is beside her. "I've been dying to do that."

Really? April had the urge to dump a plate of chow mein in Mrs. Pang's lap?

"Is she still out there?"

"No, they left, but first they asked to get the rest boxed."

Of course, they did. Why leave behind a perfectly good meal?

"I can't believe I did that."

"Well, you can't stay in there," Becca says. "We need you out here helping."

I know she's right. I can't just hide in here and let them do all the work.

"Where's Glen?"

"He's still cleaning up."

"I should help him." I struggle to my feet and look in the mirror. My eyes are red from crying. How can I go out there looking like this?

"I'll help him," April says.

"I'll take care of the other tables," Becca adds.

At least I'm no longer crying when I step out of the restroom several minutes later. I feel as if I've let my parents down. It was an accident, I tell myself, but then why do I feel so guilty? I didn't spill a plate of shrimp chow mein in Mrs. Pang's lap on purpose, did I? A small doubt nags at me. Maybe subconsciously I wanted to do it, and that's why I feel guilty.

I look out over the counter into the dining room. Glen is kneeling, wiping off a chair leg at the table where the two couples sat. April stands beside him stacking their dishes on a tray. As I watch, she rests a hand on his shoulder. He freezes for a second, then continues as if nothing just happened.

CHAPTER 23

Alec

"Hi, Alec," Eve says, a hint of a smile playing around her lips. She's wearing black pants and a pink top that clings to her breasts.

My mother shoots me a look of annoyance. Did Eve interrupt her plans for a date with Roger-Dodger? Am I to blame? Probably since obviously Eve is here because of me.

"Your mother and I were just talking about you," Eve says. "I was telling her what good friends we became at Eugene."

"What are you doing here?" I ask, not caring if it sounds rude. Whatever she's up to, it can't be good.

Her lips pout. "I thought you'd be glad to see me again."

She can't possibly believe that. She knows I couldn't wait to get away from her.

My mother clears her throat. "Miss Nielsen—Eve—was just telling me about what happened in Eugene."

I don't like the way she said that. Nothing happened in Eugene. Unless she means the fact that I shared a motel room with Eve. Maybe I shouldn't have, but what was I supposed to do? Other than that, I have no idea what this is about.

"I'm pregnant," Eve says sweetly, as if confessing it's her birthday or she just got a tattoo.

"What?" It takes a second for the shock to set in before I add, "Whose?"—although I have a feeling I know what she's going to say.

"Yours."

"You're insane."

My mother's face is expressionless. Her eyes haven't wavered from me since I walked in the door. She looks at me as if she doesn't know me.

"She's making it up," I tell my mother. "There's no way she's pregnant. I swear nothing happened."

"She wants $25,000." My mother's voice is flat.

Eve is hitting my mother up for money? Why doesn't she laugh in Eve's face? Why doesn't she tell her to leave?

"She's probably not even pregnant."

"I never dreamed you'd be so mean about this," Eve says, pouting again. "You said you loved me. If you hadn't said that, I would never have . . ." She flutters her hand and a ring on her finger catches the light. It sparkles like a small diamond.

I wonder if my mother noticed it.

"Listen, Mom, you can't believe a word she says. Nothing happened. Don't give her any money."

Eve presses a hand to her chest, pretending to be hurt. "Alec, I'm *so* disappointed. Clara thought you would do the right thing." Again that ring on her finger catches the light. A diamond ring or a cheap imitation? Does it matter?

"Clara knows about this?"

"Of course. Why else do you think she let me borrow her car?"

The black BMW in the drive belongs to Clara? I feel horrified that she has told Clara a lie like this about me. Did Clara believe her?

My mother stands up stiffly and rubs her forehead as if she has a migraine coming on. Without another word, she walks out of the room, leaving us alone.

"You've got a nerve coming here demanding money," I tell Eve. "Why are you doing this?"

"You could say you're happy to see me."

"You know I'm not."

"That's a pity."

"Are you really pregnant?"

"Why would I lie about a thing like that?"

"You know nothing happened between us."

"Oh, but it did. Have you forgotten so soon?"

"You're sick."

"That's not a very nice thing to say to the future mother of your child."

"You've got a nerve coming here asking my mother for money."

"Actually, she offered it to me."

"I don't believe you."

"No? Just ask her."

My mother walks back into the room with a grim look on her face and her checkbook in her hand.

"No, Mom, don't. It isn't true. Nothing happened. If she's pregnant, it's by someone else. I swear nothing happened."

Ignoring me, she rests her checkbook on the coffee table and starts to write out a check.

"She can't prove it. Ask her for a DNA test."

When my mother finishes, she tears out the check and hands it to Eve. "I expect this to be the end of the matter."

Eve looks at the check and smiles. Then she looks around the living room at the large screen TV, the painting of Mount Hood on the wall, the picture window framed by white curtains, and the white shag carpet on the floor. "This is a nice place you have."

I wonder what's going through her mind. Is she considering hitting my mother up for more money? Does she want the house too?

"You have what you came for, Miss Nielsen," my mother says coldly. "Now please leave."

Eve shrugs and tucks the check into her purse, a small white rectangle dangling from a slim strap she pulls over her shoulder.

"It was nice to meet you," she tells my mother, as if this was a social visit after all. I half expect her to extend a hand to shake, but apparently she thinks better of it.

I open the door for her, determined not to let her catch me off guard the way she did that day at Clara's.

She pauses in the doorway. "How's Jenny? I meant to see her too, but I guess it's a little late now." Outside it's almost dark and the streetlights are coming on.

I don't know if she means the lateness of the hour or her supposed pregnancy, but the suggestion that she might look up Jenny alarms me. Jenny has enough to worry about without Eve adding to it.

"Stay away from Jenny."

"I suppose you haven't told her yet."

"Told her what?"

"About us, of course."

"There is no us."

She lays a hand on her stomach, which as far as I can see is flat. "Of course, there is."

I watch her walk to her car. She turns before she gets in and waves to me, but I don't wave back.

Closing the door, I turn to my mother. "Why did you pay her?"

"I had no choice."

"Of course, you did. She was making it up. There never anything between us. You know how I feel about Jenny."

"Well, obviously you know this girl."

"That doesn't mean anything. She tricked me into giving her a lift from Emmett Falls to Eugene. But I swear nothing happened. Why don't you believe me?"

She sighs. "It doesn't matter what I believe. What matters is to keep her from spreading malicious slander about you all over Sutter's Bend and dragging our name through the mud."

"But it isn't true."

"Maybe not, but people would believe it all the same. What your father's doing is bad enough. I can't do anything about that. But I don't need this too."

I feel hurt that she won't believe me. I'd like to tell Jenny about Eve's visit, but what if she doesn't believe me either? I just hope that the money my mother gave Eve is the end of it.

CHAPTER 24

Jenny

When I get back from my morning jog, a black car with tinted windows is parked at the curb in front of our house. Seeing it makes me uneasy. It reminds me of a hearse, maybe because I'm worried about my mother. At any rate it seems ominous. I can't see through the windows, but as I near it, the driver's door swings open and Eve climbs out, long-legged and elegant. She's wearing a pink top, black stretch pants, and large sunglasses that hide her eyes. Her white-blonde hair hangs in a braid. She smiles at me.

"What are you doing here?" I ask, giving her a hug and then glancing at the dark windows of the car. "Is Clara here too?"

"No, she's back in Emmett Falls. I came alone. She doesn't like long road trips. They make her carsick."

"You drove all that way?"

"Sure. Why not?"

"You must be tired."

"Not really. I spent the night at the Hidey Hole. Not exactly the Hilton." She grimaces.

The Hidey Hole motel is just east of Sutter's Bend. It always looks a bit forlorn and neglected, but then Sutter's Bend doesn't attract a lot of visitors.

"You got here yesterday?"

"Yeah." She looks at our house. "Are you going to invite me in?"

"Of course."

"So you jog?" Eve says as we walk to the front door.

"Yes, it makes me feel better when I go for a run. It clears my head."

Once we're inside, she takes off her sunglasses and looks around. It's a small house but comfortable, with framed photos on the wall of our family through the years. She looks at the first couple of photos.

My father is in the living room watching a morning news show. I introduce Eve and then lead her to the kitchen, where we can talk.

"Hang on a second," I tell her. "I'll be right back. I just have to check on my mom."

I leave her sitting at the table and tiptoe to my parents' bedroom, where I crack the door open enough to see my mother is still sleeping. I don't want to disturb her, so I close it again as quietly as I can.

"How's she doing?" Eve asks when I return to the kitchen.

"She has good days and bad days."

"Which is today?"

"It's too soon to tell."

"You're so lucky to have a home like this," Eve says, looking around.

Like the rest of the house, the kitchen is old and small. The linoleum is worn, and the appliances are showing their age. It isn't nearly as nice as Clara's house, so I'm not sure what she means. Again I wonder why she's here.

"Is Clara all right?" I ask.

"Yes, she's fine."

"Does she know you're here?"

"Of course. She loaned me her car."

I glance out the window at the black car with the tinted windows parked at the curb. It seems strange a blind woman would own a car, but in a way it makes sense since she probably needs someone to drive her around or run errands for her.

Just then Becca wanders in still in her pajamas, her hair rumpled. I introduce her to Eve.

"Don't mind me," Becca says. "I just need to make some toast. I'm not awake until I've had breakfast."

"You're very lucky to have a sister," Eve tells me as Becca drops a slice of bread into the toaster. "I always wanted a sister."

"I thought you have a stepsister."

"It's not the same."

Maybe not. Then I remember she told Alec that her family died in a car accident.

"Alec said you lost your family in a car accident?"

She shrugs. "That's right. There *was* a car accident when I was a child. Just my mother and I survived."

I decide to let it go. Alec must have assumed her mother died. And even if her mother survived, it was still a tragic loss.

Becca's toast pops up. I can't tell if she's listening or not, but she seems in no hurry to leave. Her back is turned as she spreads marmalade on her toast.

Eve reaches out and touches my hand. "I just had to come see you. I couldn't go back to Emmett Falls without letting you know"—she glances at Becca's back and lowers her voice—"I'm *so* sorry."

"Sorry about what?" I wonder if she's apologizing for kissing Alec the night we left. She said the same thing that night just before she kissed him.

"Didn't he tell you?"

"Tell me what?"

"We're engaged." She holds up her left hand and wiggles her fingers. There's a small diamond ring on her finger. "We're going to be married."

I stare at the ring, not wanting to believe it. Alec and Eve engaged? Not possible.

"At least I *think* we are."

She's not sure? Did Alec give her the ring? I don't want to ask. I'm afraid she'll say yes.

"Oh, please say you're happy for me. I wanted you to be the first to know."

I wonder if she's delusional, but, no, she looks the way any girl who just got engaged would look—smiling, eyes shining, excited.

On the other hand, I feel as if the bottom just dropped out of my world and left me in free fall.

"It's just that it's so sudden," I tell her.

"Yes, it *is* sudden. It all happened so fast."

My chest feels tight. "When did it happen?"

"Last night."

She saw Alec last night?

"I told him I'm pregnant."

Pregnant? Really?

"Of course, he was surprised."

I'll bet. "You mean pregnant by Alec?"

"Yes, of course. What did you think I meant?"

I was hoping I had misunderstood. It didn't make any sense. Surely it can't be true.

"How? When?"

"That night in Eugene when we stayed at that motel. One thing just sort of led to another. Didn't he tell you?"

I feel as if someone punched me in the stomach. I knew that they had stayed at a motel. I just assumed nothing had happened. Alec didn't even *like* Eve. But maybe when they were alone at the motel . . .

In my mind I see Eve again in the entryway of Clara's house fling her arm around Alec's neck and kiss him. In the car afterward he had refused to talk about it. Maybe he was ashamed to admit what had happened between them the night before.

Suddenly I'm aware of Becca still standing there. She hasn't moved a muscle. I'm sure she's heard every word.

Eve glances at her too, as if remembering she's there.

"I thought Alec would have told you by now," Eve says.

"No, he didn't."

"Well, now you know. I hope you don't hold it against me. I want you to come to the wedding. It'll be small. Small weddings are nicer than big ones, don't you think? Maybe here in Sutter's Bend so all of Alec's friends can come."

Becca turns around and glares at her. "I don't know who you are, but if you're any kind of friend, you'd know how Jenny feels about Alec. I doubt she wants to come to your stupid wedding if what you say is true and there really is a wedding."

Eve looks startled. Her eyes fly to me. "It was just one of those things. You understand, don't you, Jenny? I didn't *mean* for anything to happen." She reaches across the table again for my hand.

I just want her to leave. I pull my hand away. How could Alec have slept with her? How could he not have told me?

"Maybe I should leave now," Eve says. "I thought you'd be happy for me."

I almost say, *I am*, but the words stick in my throat. How can I possibly be happy for her when she has just ripped my heart open?

Becca steps closer and puts her hand protectively on my shoulder. At the same moment my father appears in the doorway.

"Everything okay here?" he asks.

I wonder what sixth sense he has that tells him all is not well.

"Yeah," Becca says. "Jenny's friend is just leaving."

He nods and continues on down the short hall, probably to check on my mom.

"I didn't mean to upset you," Eve says.

Becca's hand on my shoulder tightens. She's letting me know I'm not alone. We may drive each other crazy, but we always have each other's back.

Eve sighs and slips the strap of her purse over her shoulder. "Well, I hope you'll change your mind and come to the wedding."

When I don't say anything, she turns and walks away. I listen to her footsteps recede.

"Do you believe her?" Becca says after the front door closes. "Do you think she's really engaged to Alec?"

"She has a ring," I say dully.

"That doesn't mean Alec gave it to her."

I know Becca's right, and yet what if he did? I don't know what I believe anymore.

I just assumed nothing happened that night they spent together in Eugene. Was that naive of me?

"Jenny! Becca!" Dad shouts, and Eve is forgotten in our mad dash to our parents' bedroom.

CHAPTER 25

Alec

Something's wrong. Jenny hasn't answered my texts all day. This isn't like her. It reminds me of when she ran off to Emmett Falls. Only she wouldn't do that now—not with her mother sick. So after work I drive to the Golden Duck to find out what's going on. Becca is standing just inside the door, holding several menus. Beyond her April is waiting tables. I knew April was working here, but it's still a bit of a shock to see her with her hair pinned up and wearing the white apron the others wear. Waiting tables is not the sort of job I picture her doing. Her father is on the town council, and I doubt she needs the money.

"What are you doing here?" Becca asks, glancing over her shoulder, maybe wondering what's caught my attention.

"I want to talk to Jenny. It'll only take a moment."

"She's not here. She's at the hospital. Mom got worse this morning. My dad and Jenny are both there with her."

That might explain why she hasn't texted me. If her mother has been rushed to the hospital, she must be frantic with worry.

"Any word how your Mom's doing?"

"They're still running tests."

"Do you think Jenny would mind if I went there?"

Becca's brow furrows, then clears. "Sure. Why not? Only you should know—Eve came to our house this morning."

"Eve Nielsen? What did she want?"

"Maybe you should ask Jenny."

Now I *am* worried. I thought Eve was driving back to Emmett Falls after my mother paid her off last night. She got what she came for, didn't she? Why go to Jenny? I can think of only one reason—to tell her she's pregnant. And that it's my fault. So much for my mother's effort to buy her silence. I have to find Jenny and explain. Maybe Eve is the real reason she hasn't texted.

Our hospital is a modest two-story brick building in a residential neighborhood. It's where Toby and I were born and where I've visited classmates who had their appendix out and Tyler when he had his leg in traction after falling off the roof of his house. It isn't dark yet when I get there, but the warmth of the day is waning. I don't bother to stop at the front desk but head straight for the waiting room, hoping to find Jenny there. Instead I find her father staring vacantly out a window, an open magazine lying on his lap forgotten. He doesn't notice me until I'm right in front of him. Then he blinks at me as if coming back from somewhere far away.

"How's Mrs. Chen doing?" I ask.

"They're keeping her here tonight. They thought that best. They told me I should go home, but I don't like to leave her by herself."

"I stopped by the Golden Duck. Becca said Jenny is here."

"Yes, she's in the cafeteria. I told her to go find something to eat."

"Did you get something to eat?"

"I'm not really hungry."

I feel sorry for him. He looks lost sitting by himself in the nearly empty room. There are just two other people—a man and woman near the door talking in low voices.

"I'll see if I can find Jenny," I tell him.

He nods and turns back to the window, where the streetlights have just come on.

I take an elevator to the second floor and follow the signs to the cafeteria. A small number of people sit singly and in small clusters around the room, and the food service is closed now. Jenny sits alone at a table by the window with a bottle of water and a half-finished sandwich, reading a book propped open in front of her.

When I walk over to her, she looks up and gives me a half-hearted smile. "How did you know where to find me?"

"I saw your father downstairs. He said you were here."

She lifts a hand to her forehead and closes her eyes. Then she opens them again.

"Are you okay?"

"It's been a rough day."

"How's your mom doing?"

"She's resting. They gave her some sort of vitamins in her IV. They said she was dehydrated and had a low white blood cell count. I thought . . . " Her lip quivers.

I reach across and squeeze her hand. "I went by the Duck. Becca said Eve came to see you this morning."

201

"I don't want to talk about it."

"Whatever she told you, it's a lie."

"She said you're getting married."

"*What?*" Not what I was expecting. Why would Eve say we're getting married? But then why would Eve say anything. She's a troublemaker and a pathological liar. "Don't tell me you believed her?"

"She had a ring."

"Yeah, I know. She came to our house last night. She got my mom to write her a check for $25,000."

Jenny frowns. "Why?"

"To keep quiet."

"About what?"

I shift uncomfortably, unable to look her in the eye and repeat Eve's outrageous lie.

"She said she's pregnant," Jenny says quietly.

"Yeah. That's what she told us too. It's not true, of course."

"She said you slept with her that night at the motel in Eugene."

"I didn't. I swear I didn't."

Jenny sighs. "It doesn't matter."

"What do you mean it doesn't matter? It matters to me. You have to believe me. I don't know why she's doing this. I don't think she even likes me very much. If she thinks she's going to get more money from my mom, she's wrong. Look, you've got to believe me."

"You didn't give her the ring?"

"No, of course not. She probably bought it for herself. I tell you, she's crazy."

"I wonder if Clara knows what she's up to."

"She said Clara loaned her the car."

"She told me that too. You don't suppose Clara is in any danger, do you?"

"Why do you say that?"

"Maybe Eve stole the car. Maybe she ran off and left Clara with no one to take care of her."

I picture Clara in her wheelchair in the sunroom blindly staring out at her garden. Would Eve go off and just leave her? When we went to Eugene, at least she had arranged for Mrs. Duncan to stay with Clara.

"We could call," Jenny says, pulling out her phone. I watch her enter the number and then hear it ringing at the other end. She frowns. "No one answers. It's going to voicemail."

Of course, that doesn't mean Clara's in any danger. Maybe no one could get to the phone and pick up before it went to voicemail.

Jenny bites her lip. "I hope she's okay. Maybe we should check on her."

"How?"

"Go there. See if she's okay."

"It's a long drive. What about your mother?"

Jenny's face falls. "Could you go?"

"I could, but I'd have to be back for work tomorrow." I don't add that Eve is probably back in Emmett Falls by now, and I'd just as soon avoid her if I can.

"Forget it. It was just a thought."

I feel like I've let her down, but before I can say more, her father appears in the doorway. She grabs her book, the half-eaten sandwich, and the bottle of water. I follow her as she dashes across the room.

"Your mother's awake," he tells her. "She wants to talk to you."

Jenny drops what's left of her sandwich in the nearest trash bin.

He glances at me. "Only one person can go in at a time."

"You'll wait for me, won't you?" she asks, touching my arm.

"Of course."

Her father and I trudge back to the waiting room together. I sit down on the chair next to him, feeling awkward. The couple who were sitting by the door are gone now and we're alone. I can't think of anything to say, and so the silence stretches out between us like a gaping black hole.

After a while he sighs. "It's very hard. We've been married twenty years."

Twenty years seems like a lifetime to me. In fact, it's probably how long my parents have been married. And now they're getting divorced.

"I remember the night I sat in this very room waiting for Jenny to be born," her father says. He smiles at the memory and shakes his head. "She's a lot like her mother—strong, you know?"

I do. Jenny is one of the strongest people I know.

"It's been hard for her having to give up her plans for college in the fall. I know she doesn't like working at the Golden Duck. It's a disappointment for her after looking forward so long to going off to college. She was always at the top of her class. And then this happened." He shakes his head again. "We never know what the future holds in store for us."

I think again of my parents and their impending divorce. I saw it coming, but I didn't really believe it would happen. Not to my family.

"What about you, Alec?" he asks. "Are you going off to college in the fall?"

"I think so."

"Good. Make something of yourself. I never had that opportunity. Not that I'm complaining. My parents did the best they could for me and my brothers. One's a dentist in Portland. The other's a chiropractor in San Francisco. I got the Golden Duck, and it's given us a decent living. My father had very little when he came from China, and he and my mother worked hard so we could have something more."

Silence falls again. I notice my knee jiggling and try to sit still. I'd leave but Jenny asked me to wait.

"What will you study at college?" he asks.

If I tell him I haven't decided, he'll think I'm not serious about my education. "My parents want me to study premed."

"A doctor. Good choice. Doctors make good money. My son Paul is studying to be a doctor." I hear the pride in his voice.

My conscience stirs uncomfortably. I feel like I'm not being honest if I let him think I'm going into premed.

"Actually, I'm not sure I want to be a doctor."

He's looking out the window again at the streetlights as a car passes. Maybe he didn't hear me. He seems lost in his thoughts.

Soon Jenny is back, a little breathless. I wonder if she took the stairs and ran all the way. Her eyes are bright and her cheeks flushed.

"She wants to talk to you."

"Me?"

"Come on."

We hold hands as we run back down the corridor to the elevator. We have the elevator to ourselves and share a quick kiss before the doors slide open with a ding.

"Why does she want to talk to me?" I ask Jenny.

"I don't know."

We're running again. We slow as we near the room where her mother lies in a hospital bed with an IV in her arm. I feel nervous as I enter. Jenny waits outside since only one of us can go in.

"Come closer." Mrs. Chen looks tired as she lies propped against a pillow.

I sit down on the chair beside her bed, wishing I could jump back up and let Jenny be there instead. Why does her mother want to talk to me?

"Is Jenny waiting by the door?" she asks.

"Yes, do you want me to get her?"

"Tell her not to stand there listening. This is private, just you and me."

I hesitate and then go to the door as she asked. Jenny is standing a few steps away, leaning against the wall. She straightens and looks expectant when she sees me.

"She doesn't want you to listen."

Jenny rolls her eyes but moves a little farther away.

I return to my chair, wondering what her mother wants to say to me that she doesn't want Jenny to hear.

"Is she there?"

"Yes, but she won't listen."

Mrs. Chen looks unconvinced. "Move closer."

I can't move my chair any closer, but I lean toward her so she can feel like I'm at least making an effort.

"I always thought I would be there for my Jenny's wedding."

I don't know what I was expecting, but not this. I try to reassure her. "I'm sure you'll be there for her wedding."

"Maybe. Maybe not. More and more, I'm not so sure."

I start to protest.

She waves her hand for silence. "Please, let me talk. I thought she would marry Glen. I thought, if I can't be there, his parents will be there for her. She'll be okay."

I wonder if she's going to ask me to break up with Jenny. My heart beats faster. I glance at the doorway, half hoping Jenny is listening after all and will rush in to rescue me. What am I supposed to say?

"But now Glen is gone and there is you."

Is she blaming me for their breakup? "We didn't intend . . . It just happened."

She waves her hand again. "Since she was a little girl, Jenny has wanted to be a scientist. She asked for her first chemistry set for Christmas when she was seven. I thought, what is this? Why doesn't she still want dolls? But, no, she wanted a chemistry set. She was quite insistent about that. Nothing else would do."

I can't help wondering where this is going. At least she's not still talking about Glen.

"All her life Jenny has wanted to be a scientist."

"I know."

"I want you to promise me—" She closes her eyes.

I feel a moment of panic. *Promise what?*

Her eyes fly open again. "Jenny's future is important. If you and Jenny decide to marry, I want you to promise to help her."

"I will. I promise."

"Have your parents met Jenny?"

I glance at the doorway again. How much has Jenny told her about my parents? No, they haven't met Jenny, but that's because my father is in Toronto having an affair with a woman we've never met and my mother thinks Jenny isn't good enough for me.

"Just as I thought. We met you, but your parents haven't met Jenny. Why not? Because you know they won't approve of her?"

"No. It's not like that," I say uneasily.

"Then how is it? Will they accept Jenny or not? Because if they don't, they'll try to turn you against her. Jenny deserves more."

"Yes, she does. I agree. But please don't ask me to give her up because of my parents. I can't help how they think. And they're getting divorced. Jenny's the only thing in my life that makes sense right now."

"Divorced? Jenny didn't tell me this."

"My dad's in Canada. He went off to a conference more than a month ago, and we haven't seen him since. My mom says he's got a girlfriend there. He won't answer my phone calls and ignores most of my texts. My mom's dating this guy I can't stand. I feel like I have to go off to college so I don't have to stay here and watch."

I know I should keep all this family dysfunction to myself, but I can't seem to help myself. It pours out like hot lava from a volcano that just won't quit.

"They want me to study premed, but I know I'll hate it. The thing is, I don't know what I want to do. I'm not like Jenny. I haven't known since I was seven what I want to be."

I stop, feeling guilty for having unburdened myself to a woman who has enough to worry about right now without me dumping all my problems on her.

"Sorry," I mutter.

"There's nothing wrong with not knowing what you want to do. You're young. You just haven't found it yet. But you will. Be patient. Now, have you told your mother how you feel about this new man in her life?"

The question surprises me. "Yes, but she doesn't listen to me."

"Maybe you should try to look at him through her eyes. Ask her what she likes about him. Sometimes it helps us understand if we try to see things from someone else's point of view. Now I think I need to rest. But first I want to talk to Jenny. Can you send her in before you leave?"

She closes her eyes again, as if she's used up all her strength talking to me. She looks fragile lying there hooked up to an IV and a monitoring screen. I wish I could do something for her. It must be frightening knowing you might be dying.

Jenny is leaning against the wall reading her book when I step out of the room. She looks up and closes her book. "What did she say?"

"She asked if my parents have met you."

"Did you tell her they're getting divorced?"

"I think I thoroughly ruined her impression of me."

She grins. "I doubt that. You don't know my mom."

"Now it's your turn."

She puts her hand on my arm. "You should go home."

"What about you?"

"I'm going to stay as long as the nurses will let me."

She kisses my cheek before slipping into her mother's room.

I stand there a few more minutes listening to the low murmur of their voices before I leave.

The next morning I decide to take Mrs. Chen's advice and try again to talk to my mom about Roger-Dodger. I get up early to catch her before Toby comes down for breakfast.

When I walk into the kitchen, she's dressed for the office in a grey suit and a white shirt, measuring ground coffee into the coffeemaker.

"You're up early," she says.

"I wanted to talk to you about Roger."

"What about him?"

"I'm trying to understand what you see in him."

"Oh, really?"

"I'm serious."

She sighs. "So why are you asking me this?"

"Because I'm trying to understand."

"Okay, if you really want to know, for starters, he's dependable."

She means compared to Dad, who's shacked up with a woman in Toronto.

"How's he dependable?" I ask.

"He'd be there for me. That's what I mean."

Dad again.

"You don't know that. You hardly know the guy."

"Honestly, Alec, my personal life is none of your business."

"It is if you're going to marry him."

"Who said anything about marrying? And if it comes to that, I think it's *my* business who I marry."

"What about Toby and me? Don't we get any say in this?"

"The last time I heard, you're going away to college in the fall, and I'm certainly not going to have a nine-year-old telling me who I can date."

"I think he's got a right to have a voice in this. He could end up having Roger-Dodger for a dad."

"Listen, it's too early in the morning for this conversation. And stop calling him that."

"Just tell me one more thing you like about him."

"All right. He makes me feel desirable. Does that satisfy you? Now go wake your brother up. I don't want to be late for work."

Well, I tried. I think about what she said as I tromp up the stairs. He's dependable and he makes her feel desirable. Dependable, I get. It's that second one that bothers me. I'm not used to thinking of my mother as desirable. She's my mom. Moms aren't supposed to be desirable. At least not the way she means. Maybe that's one of the reasons I don't like Roger-Dodger. Okay, so he makes her feel desirable and she's probably lonely, but understanding that doesn't make me feel any better about how he's worming his way into our family.

I knock on Toby's door and then nudge it open. "Hey, pal, time to get up."

Toby groans, sits up, and stretches. His clothes are all laid out neatly on a chair near his bed. All he has to do is put them on.

My mission accomplished, I head back to my room to retrieve my phone. A quick look tells me I have a couple of missed calls and a text from Dustin. I read the text first. *Dude, check this out.* A link takes me to a post by Eve that accuses me of getting her pregnant and trying to buy her off with $25,000. The list of comments goes on and on. I feel sick as I scroll down through them. Total strangers sympathize with her and think I'm a louse. There isn't anything I can do about it.

"So is it true?" Dustin asks when I call him.

"Of course, it isn't true. At least not the part about me getting her pregnant. It was my mom's bright idea to pay her $25,000."

"Why'd your mom do that if it wasn't true?"

"She thought she could make it go away."

"Looks like she was wrong."

I just hope it blows over quickly. At least Jenny knows about Eve's claim. That's one small consolation.

After calling Dustin, I try to phone Jenny to warn her about the post. My call goes to voicemail. Maybe she's sleeping in or maybe she's gone back to the hospital to be with her mother. I'll try again later. In the meantime I send her a text.

A half hour later when I show up for work at the Bookery, Mrs. Kilmer glares at me from behind the counter with more than her usual disapproval. I ignore her and head for the boxes of books that need to be unpacked and shelved before we open.

Liv looks up from the box she's working on. *"They know,"* she whispers.

"Know what?"

"About the pregnant girlfriend."

"She's not my girlfriend and she's not pregnant."

"Well, tell that to the internet."

Dave emerges from his office, no doubt alerted by Mrs. Kilmer that I've arrived. He looks grim as he walks toward me.

"I can explain," I say quickly, hoping to ward off what I fear is coming.

"Someone posted it on the comments section of our website," he growls.

The Bookery website is his pride and joy. Every negative customer comment cuts him to the quick.

"Sorry."

"Sorry isn't good enough."

"I swear I didn't get anyone pregnant. The girl who posted that is just doing this to smear me."

"Well, then maybe you should talk to her and get it sorted out. In the meantime take some time off."

"You're firing me?"

"I haven't decided if you're fired, but you're taking a leave starting right now. Without pay."

"But what she claims isn't true."

"I don't care if it's true or not. I care what people think. This is a small town. I can't afford to lose customers."

Since arguing is unlikely to change his mind and may cause him to make my time off permanent, it's probably best if I just leave.

Mrs. Kilmer, standing behind the counter, has a smug look on her face as I exit the store. Once outside, I try to think what to do next. Then I remember Jenny's suggestion about driving to Emmett Falls and checking on Clara. Now that I have the time free, I might as well. If Eve is there, I can give her a piece of my mind. She has a lot of nerve claiming I got her pregnant. What does she hope to achieve? If she thinks I'm going to marry her, she's crazy. It's not going to happen. I want Clara to know what she did. If Eve loses her job, it's no more than she deserves. Let her see how it feels.

CHAPTER 26

Jenny

My mother is sleeping. I shift on my chair and try not to wake her. The nurses let me stay last night even though it's against the rules. I didn't get much sleep, but then I think she didn't either with all the interruptions to check her vitals or adjust what they are giving her in the IV.

I had a lot of time last night to think and found myself thinking about Malcolm's research and Clara's advice not to be too quick to decide what I want to focus on in the sciences. It came to me all at once what I want to focus on. Sitting here beside my mother, feeling so helpless, I've been telling myself there has to be a way to defeat cancer. That's what I want to focus on—cancer research.

My mother stirs. Her eyes open and she smiles. "Jenny." Her voice is hoarse.

I reach out and hold her hand. It feels so thin and fragile, and I try to blink back my tears.

"Have you been here all night?" she asks.

"Yes. They let me stay."

"You should go home and get some sleep."

"I will when Dad gets here."

"I'm so sorry all this happened. I feel bad about it. You should be getting ready to go to college."

"College can wait."

"Are you sure?"

"I'm sure." And it's true. College will still be waiting when all of this is over. But my time with my mother may be limited. It's funny how my perspective has shifted so much in such a short time. It no longer seems like the end of the world if I don't start classes in the fall.

"Did you get any sleep last night?" she asks.

"A little."

"You didn't have to stay."

"I know, but I wanted to."

My mother looks up at the ceiling. "I like Alec. He's a nice boy."

"I like him too."

She looks at me. "I want you to be happy. You know that, don't you?"

"I know. I will be."

We are interrupted by a young orderly with dark curly hair and tattoos on his arms who has come to transport her for an MRI. After she's gone, two aides ask me to step outside while they change her sheets.

In the hallway I check my phone for messages and find a text from Alec. Eve has posted on Facebook that he got her pregnant. I don't understand why she would do this. Just yesterday she was insisting they were going to get married. And I believed her, although I don't know why. I should never have doubted Alec for a second. I wonder if she's in love with him.

If she is, she has a funny way of showing it. Does she think she can somehow pressure him into marrying her?

I have a text from Megan too, wanting to know if I've seen Eve's post. It seems to be spreading like wildfire. I don't bother to click on the link. What would be the point? Right now I couldn't care less what Eve posts.

Then I see a text from Eve. My finger hovers over it, but I decide not to open it. Anything she has to say to me can wait. I have more important things to worry about.

CHAPTER 27

Alec

During the long ride to Emmett Falls I rehearse in my head what I'll say to Eve when I see her. But it's hard to stay angry for so long. By the time I get there, I've calmed down considerably and even begun to regret that I made the trip at all. It seems unlikely Eve would do anything to hurt Clara. And I doubt anything I say to her will make her feel remorse for the lie she told about me. But after driving so far, I can't just turn around and go back to Sutter's Bend without checking on Clara after I told Jenny I would.

I'm prepared to confront Eve when the door opens, but instead it's Mrs. Duncan who stands before me. She breaks into a broad smile. "Alec. This is a surprise. Come in. Clara will be tickled pink to see you." She holds the door open for me, and I step into the cool dim hallway with the photographs of flowers on the walls.

"Is Eve here?" I ask.

"I'm afraid not. Did you drive all this way to see her?"

Too late I realize it might look as if I'm pursuing Eve when that could not be farther from the truth. "Actually, no.

It's Clara I came to see. Jenny tried to phone her yesterday, and no one answered. We were worried she might need help. We thought Eve might have gone off and left her alone."

"Eve isn't here, that's true, but I am. Everything's fine. I'm sorry you felt you had to drive all that way. I think I know why we didn't get your call. Our phone was out of order for a while. Somehow it got unplugged. I don't know how that happened. As soon as I noticed, I plugged it right back in."

I wonder if Eve deliberately unplugged the phone before she left, but I decide to keep that to myself.

"Have you had lunch?" Mrs. Duncan asks.

"Yes, I stopped along the way." This isn't true, but I don't want her to feel she has to feed me.

"Nothing's wrong I hope?"

"I don't think so. I just need to talk to Mrs. Weisberger. It's about Eve."

"Clara's in the sunroom. She likes to sit there this time of day. We open the door, and she can hear the birds in the garden and smell the roses. She does love that garden."

I follow her to the sunroom, where Clara sits in her wheelchair facing the sliding glass doors and the garden. The glass doors stand open, and only a screen separates us from the outdoors.

"Here's Alec, Jenny's friend, come all this way from Sutter's Bend to see you," Mrs. Duncan says.

"What a nice surprise." Clara holds out her hand, and I step forward to take it. "Jenny's not with you?"

"No, she couldn't come. Her mother's in the hospital."

"And how is she doing?"

"The doctors say they have to wait and see. Jenny's worried, of course."

"Poor thing. Of course, she is. I wish there was something I could do."

Mrs. Duncan pulls a chair closer for me and then seats herself on another.

"So Eve's not here?" I ask.

"I'm afraid not," Clara says. "We haven't seen her for several days, have we, Mavis?"

"No, we have not, and that's a fact," says Mrs. Duncan.

"Do you know where she is?" I ask, looking from one to the other.

"No, she didn't say where she was going," says Clara.

"Well, I can tell you where she went. Sutter's Bend."

Clara frowns. "Oh?"

"She said you loaned her your car."

"I let her borrow it from time to time. It's just sitting there in the garage gathering dust. I don't mind if she takes it for a spin now and again. Generally she doesn't go far."

Sutter's Bend is hardly a spin, but I let it pass. However, Clara should know what Eve has been up to.

"She showed up at my house two days ago and told my mother I got her pregnant. She persuaded my mother to give her $25,000."

"Oh, dear," Clara says, dismayed.

"And that's not all. She showed up at Jenny's house yesterday and told her we're going to get married."

"Married?" Mrs. Duncan looks puzzled. "Why on earth would she say that?"

"I don't know, but I wish she'd stop. Do you have any idea why she's doing this?"

"Eve . . . has episodes," Clara says slowly.

"Episodes?"

"Usually they blow over. Sometimes she disappears for a few days, but she always comes back."

"She's done things like this before?"

"Not exactly like this."

"Is she dangerous?"

"I don't think so. She's never hurt anyone. Even her mother says . . ."

"I thought her mother was dead."

"No, she's very much alive."

"They live here in Emmett Falls," Mrs. Duncan says, leaning forward. "Her mother's active in the local arts community."

"There was the business about the fire," Clara says, "but no one ever proved anything."

"A fire?"

"Her parents' house. It could have been an accident, but no one knows for sure. Eve was angry at her mother at the time. A neighbor saw the flames and turned a garden hose on it until the fire department arrived. The damage was minimal. No real harm done."

"Aren't you worried she might do something like that again?"

"I thought I could help her by giving her a job. And as I said, no one knows for sure what happened."

At that moment I notice the same tall young man I saw in the garden on my first visit. He stands among the flowers with a pair of garden shearers in his hands, apparently unaware that he has an audience. As I watch, he wipes the sweat from his forehead with the back of his arm.

"There's a man out there," I say in surprise.

"That's Carl," Mrs. Duncan tells me.

"I have him to thank for my lovely garden," says Clara. "He has a true green thumb."

"I just wasn't expecting to see someone out there."

"Carl's a friend of Eve's. She's the one who found him. I think they met last year at that place in Nevada where they have a bonfire each year."

"Burning Man."

"Yes, that's the one."

"Do you think he might know where she is?"

"You could ask him."

"All right, I will."

I stand and push open one of the screens and step out into the garden. The man with the shearers turns his head and looks at me.

"I hear you're a friend of Eve's," I say. "By any chance do you know where she is?"

"Who are you?"

"Alec Morrissey."

He shows no sign of recognizing my name, just squints at the sun. "Don't know. She could be anywhere. Eve's a free spirit you might say."

"Yeah, I just thought you might . . ."

He squats among the flowers again, as if he has said all he intends to say. If he knows where she is, he's not telling.

When I go back inside, Clara and Mrs. Duncan are talking in low voices.

"Tell him," Clara says.

"Tell me what?" I look from one to the other.

"We thought you should know . . . ," Mrs. Duncan begins. "It might not mean anything."

"Know what?"

She hesitates. "There's a gun missing."

I stare at her, a sinking feeling in the pit of my stomach. "A gun? You think Eve took it?"

"We don't know. Maybe it just got mislaid."

Mislaid. Right. I glance back at the garden. Eve missing. A gun missing. Is it a coincidence?

"I don't think she would *do* anything," Clara says. "Maybe she took it for protection."

Mrs. Duncan avoids my eyes, keeping her opinion to herself. Maybe she doesn't want to contradict Clara.

So where is Eve? I ask myself. And then a cold chill slithers down my spine as it occurs to me that maybe she's still in Sutter's Bend.

CHAPTER 28

Jenny

When I get home from the hospital, I lie down and promptly fall asleep. It's two in the afternoon when I wake. Checking my phone, I find a text from Alec telling me he lost his job at the Bookery as a result of Eve's post and is on his way to Emmett Falls to check on Clara. By now he could be there. I text him—*Where are you?*—knowing he may be out of range of a signal if he's on the road. Then I ride my bike back to the hospital to check on my mom. She's doing better and doesn't want me to miss another night's sleep, so I start home before dark. On the way I ride by Alec's house to see if he's home yet. There are lights on in the house but no sign of his car, so he's probably not back. On impulse I decide to stop anyway and ask his mother if she's heard from him.

I've hardly had time to ring the bell when Toby throws the door open. His face lights up when he sees me. In the background I hear his mother calling, wanting to know who's at the door.

"It's Jenny," he shouts back.

A moment later she appears behind him, still dressed for the office. It's the first time we've met face-to-face, although I've seen her at school events.

"Alec's not here," she says.

"I know. I thought you might have heard from him."

"Aside from a text saying he was going, no. I don't know why he wasn't at work today. I thought maybe he was with you."

It sounds like an accusation, as if I'm somehow to blame for his not being home. I tell myself maybe she's had a hard day. Or then again maybe she just doesn't like me.

But she's Alec's mother, so I make an effort to be polite. "He sent me a text too. I don't think he worked today. I think they let him go."

"Oh, not again! Honestly, what is with my son and gainful employment?"

This strikes me as unfair, and I leap to Alec's defense. "It wasn't his fault. It was Eve. She posted something about him that went viral."

"After I paid her off? You've got to be kidding."

Toby taps her arm. "Can Jenny stay with me while you go out with Roger-Dodger?"

"Don't call him that. And I'm sure she's busy."

Toby's face falls.

"I would, but I'm really tired," I tell him. "I didn't get much sleep last night."

Alec's mother glances at her watch. "I don't even know if Roger is coming over tonight. I haven't heard from him all day." She frowns. "Oh, you might as well come in."

It isn't exactly a warm invitation, but I decide I'm not going to let her intimidate me.

"Maybe just for a minute."

She notices my bike leaning against the wall of the garage and quirks an eyebrow. "Isn't it rather late to be out on your bike?"

"I was just on my way home from the hospital."

Mention of the hospital elicits a fleeting look of embarrassment. "How is your mother doing?"

"I think they'll let her come home soon. They have a new drug they're going to try—if she can tolerate it."

When I step into the house, Toby grabs my hand and we follow his mother into the living room. I hesitate before stepping on the white carpet. I hope I'm not tracking in dirt. She seats herself in a large armchair while Toby and I settle ourselves on the sofa across from her. Between us is a glass-top coffee table holding a vase of yellow tulips. A large screen TV is mounted on the wall to our left, and a painting of Mount Hood hangs on the wall behind me. Behind Alec's mother white curtains with gold tassels frame a large window that looks out on the street. I glance down at my sneakers again, wondering if I ought to have removed them before stepping on the carpet.

"I suppose Alec told you about his father?" she asks.

Probably she's referring to the fact that he's in Canada with another woman. Or maybe the divorce.

"Yes."

"Toby, go watch TV upstairs."

"Do I have to?"

"Or play a video game."

"Minecraft?"

"Okay."

"Yes!"

After he races up the stairs, she sighs. "We've been married almost twenty years and now this."

"I'm sorry."

"I don't know what I'm supposed to do. I don't know who I am anymore. Everyone tells me I'm strong and I'll get through this, but some days . . ." She shakes her head and wipes a tear from the corner of her eye with the tip of a finger. "Some days I just want to scream."

I regret having come in because now there's no easy way to leave. I wasn't expecting her to confide in me. What am I supposed to say?

"I tell myself I can do this, but can I? What do I know about being divorced? One son headed off to college and the other in fourth grade. It's not like I can just go back to being twenty-one and single. I don't know how to do this."

I glance toward the doorway. "I should be going."

"Sorry. I didn't mean to talk about my problems. I'm sure you want to get home."

"Will you be all right?" I ask, not wanting to leave her alone if she needs someone to talk to but also not eager to stay and listen to her marital troubles.

She waves a hand. "Yes, I'll be fine. You know, I'm glad we talked. I have to admit I thought Alec was making a mistake when I found out he was dating you. But you seem like a sensible girl. Maybe you're what he needs. I confess I wasn't exactly thrilled when that girl showed up here the other day claiming she was pregnant."

"You mean Eve?"

"Yes, Eve Nielsen. The thing is, I believed her. I thought, isn't that just like Alec—screwing up his life—and not giving a thought to the future. Did he tell you I gave her a check for $25,000? One more stupid decision on my part. I should have known she'd just take the money and go on causing trouble."

"I don't know why she's doing this."

She gives me a shrewd look. "Do you think she's pregnant?"

"Alec says nothing happened, and I believe him."

Somewhere in the house a phone rings.

"Maybe that's him." She jumps up and hurries out of the room to answer it. A moment later she's back, scowling, holding the phone out to me. "It's for you."

"For me?" I can't imagine why someone would call me on her phone. No one knows I'm here. I take the phone from her warily and hold it to my ear. "Hello?"

"Jenny, it's me."

Every muscle in my body tenses as I recognize Eve's voice. Her timing is uncanny. It's as if she knew we were talking about her.

"What do you want?"

"We need to talk."

"About what?"

"Look, can we meet somewhere? How about at your house?"

I feel uncomfortable about having her over after the last time. I'd rather meet somewhere more public if we're going to meet. "How about the Shack?" I suggest.

"Okay. In about ten or fifteen minutes?"

"Sure."

At least at the Shack we won't be alone, and I can walk away if I need to.

"It was Eve," I tell Alec's mother as I hand back the phone.

"Eve Nielsen? I can't believe she had the gall to call here. What did she want?"

"She wants to meet and talk."

"After what she's done, you should have nothing to do with her."

"I just thought—"

"How did she know you were here?"

"I don't know. Maybe she thought Alec would answer."

"She didn't ask for him. She asked for you."

"Maybe she wants to apologize."

"People like that don't apologize."

She may be right, but I feel I should give Eve a chance to explain.

All the same, I can't help wondering how Eve knew where to find me. Was it a lucky guess? Or did she *know*? Because if she *knew*, I can think of only one explanation. She must be watching me. And that's a disturbing thought.

As I climb on my bike, I look around uneasily for the black hearse-like car with the tinted windows that Eve was driving yesterday, but I don't see it. It's dark now. An SUV cruises past. I promise myself I'll keep the meeting short and go straight home afterward.

When I walk in the Shack, it's brightly lit and noisy. I find a table and sit down to wait for Eve to arrive. A loud group occupies one of the booths, but they are far enough away that we can ignore them. I wonder what she wants to talk about. Whatever it is, this time I won't fall for any of her lies about Alec. What she's doing has to stop. I have to make her see that it's hurtful and wrong.

When ten minutes pass and Eve still hasn't shown up, I go to the counter and order a Coke. Maybe she's changed her mind about meeting me. I'll wait another ten minutes, and if she hasn't come by then, I'll leave.

I'm about to give up when she walks in. She's wearing a black windbreaker and black pants that set off her milk-white skin and white-blonde hair. I'm sure she sees me, but she's in no rush to join me. She goes to the counter first and then wanders over with a cup of coffee in her hand.

"How did you know I was at Alec's house?" I ask.

She shrugs. "I called your house. You didn't answer. Where else would you be?"

It sounds reasonable. Maybe I was being paranoid thinking she followed me to Alec's house.

"So where's Alec?" She looks about as if he might be there, maybe sitting in one of the booths.

"Emmett Falls."

She looks surprised. "Why?"

"He went to check on Clara."

"That's a long way to go to check on her. Are you sure he wasn't looking for me?"

I don't rise to the bait. I'm not going to let her upset me.

"Did you know he lost his job today—thanks to you?"

She dismisses this news with a wave of her hand. "He'll get another one."

I notice she isn't wearing the ring. Does that mean she's given up her fantasy of marrying Alec? Maybe best not to ask. I won't bring it up if she doesn't.

"What did you want to talk about?" I ask warily.

"I wanted you to know—no hard feelings."

I watch her sip her coffee, those pouting lips and the little line that forms between her brows when she frowns.

"What do you mean?"

A shrug. "You won."

I assume she means Alec, as if he's a prize in a contest we're engaged in.

When I don't respond, she leans forward, her gaze intent. "Do you know what it's like to have never been loved? I mean, *never*. Not by the parents who are supposed to care about you. Not by a significant other. No one."

Is she trying to make me feel sorry for her?

"Maybe they didn't know how to show it."

Her eyes narrow. "You think you know me, but you don't. You know nothing about me. Nothing."

Her eyes brim with tears. And then they're streaming down her face, just as they did that day at the Pancake House in Eugene when Alec said he would buy a bus ticket for her to go back to Emmett Falls.

"Eve—please." I glance around in embarrassment.

She doesn't seem to care if anyone notices.

"That day you showed up at Clara's, and we talked—I thought you understood. I thought we could be friends." She shakes her head. "I just wanted you to like me. You had everything."

"Everything? How do I have everything?"

"You're smart. Clara likes you. You have Alec. I just wanted to be part of that." She wipes away the tears with the back of her hand.

"Eve, I don't have everything. You must see that. My family doesn't have enough money to send me to college. My mother may be dying."

She shakes her head again. "Listen, remember how we talked that night you stayed at Clara's? Remember how you told me about your first kiss with Alec?"

She has stopped crying. I wonder if she expects me to offer her a place to sleep. She must know I won't. Not after all she's done. Is she still staying at the Hidey Hole? Will she be all right when she goes back there? Surely she doesn't plan to drive all the way back to Emmett Falls tonight.

Her hand shoots out and grabs my wrist. "Show me where you and Alec first kissed, that place by the water you told me about, and I promise I'll go away and you'll never see me again."

I try to pull my hand away, but she doesn't let go.

"You're hurting my wrist."

"Then stop pulling."

"Why do you want to see it?"

I don't want to take her down by the rocks, especially not in the dark. Even in daylight it's not an easy descent.

"*Please.* I just want to see what it's like."

I know I should refuse, but if it would mean that she would go away and leave us alone . . . And I wouldn't have to take her down by the rocks. I could just show her from the road.

"If I do, will you swear that you'll go away? And you'll stop telling everyone Alec got you pregnant? Because you know that's not true."

She smiles through her tears. "Cross my heart and hope to die," she says, as if we are kids making a pact.

We set off in Clara's black BMW after loading my bike in the trunk. I'm uneasy about taking Eve to the rocks, but I feel like I have to now that I said I would. At least her mood has improved. She's chatty now and seems happy as she drives. You wouldn't guess she was in tears just a little while ago.

On the outskirts of town I tell her where to turn to get to the road that runs along the shore.

"By the way, I like your restaurant," she says after we have made the turn.

I glance at her. Eyes focused straight ahead, a hint of a smile. "You've been to the Golden Duck?"

"Well, I didn't *eat* there. I just went there. I was looking for you."

"When was this?"

"Earlier," she says vaguely.

I turn this over in my mind. If she went there earlier today, did someone tell her I was at the hospital? Did she go there, wait for me to come out, and follow me to Alec's house? I feel a twinge of panic, but I tell myself again that I'm being paranoid. Why would Eve go to such lengths to find me?

"I'm sorry I've been so awful," Eve says. "I thought Alec cared about me after that night we spent together, but I guess I was wrong."

I stay silent. I don't want to argue about what did or didn't happen that night. I'm not going to let her sow doubts in my mind about Alec.

The road twists and turns before us in the beams of our headlights, but otherwise we're surrounded by darkness.

"We're almost there," I tell her when yet another curve sign looms into view. "You can park on the shoulder of the road."

After she has pulled off, we climb out. A ghostly moon hangs over the ocean. I feel a few sprinkles on my face, and the wind whips my hair in my eyes.

"There it is." I point down at the rocky patch of shoreline in the moonlight. We can hear the waves breaking on the rocks, but there's not much to see except the black boulders squatting on the shoreline like ancient life forms.

"How do we get down?" Eve asks.

"Oh, it's too dangerous in the dark."

"But wasn't it dark when Alec took you down?"

"Yes, but he knows the trail. I don't. At least not in the dark."

"I'm sure we can figure it out. I'll bring a flashlight." The overhead light in the car goes on when she opens the car door. After fishing a flashlight from the glove compartment, she shines it over the edge of the road shoulder where the land drops away.

I thought she would be satisfied seeing the rocky strip of beach from the road. I really don't want to try to go down that steep incline in the dark without Alec.

"It's starting to rain," I point out, hoping that will discourage her.

"You can stay up here if you like, but I'm going down," she calls over her shoulder.

She aims her flashlight down the near vertical drop and looks as if she's about to launch herself over the edge, but it's not where the trail begins, and she'll probably sprain an ankle or break her neck if she strikes out blindly.

"Not there. Farther down," I say reluctantly.

"Where? Show me."

I lead her a few yards farther along the road and point out where the trail begins. She plays the beam of her flashlight over the dirt and rocks. The trail is barely visible, but that doesn't stop her.

"Okay. Who goes first?"

"I will." At least I've found my way down it by daylight. I probably have a better chance of finding the footholds than she does. She follows close behind, the beam of her flashlight bouncing off the rocks. We proceed slowly, slipping and sliding as we inch our way down.

When we reach the bottom without mishap, I feel enormously relieved. Above us at the edge of the embankment, I can just make out the dark outline of Clara's car.

"Does anyone else besides you and Alec know about this place?" Eve asks, looking about.

"I don't know. Probably."

She walks toward the boulders and the water. "Where were you when he kissed you?"

"Near that rock." I point to the smaller of the two largest boulders.

She walks toward it and I follow, the crash of the waves against the rocks louder now.

"We should go back. It's going to rain."

She doesn't seem to hear. She hugs herself. "It's just the way I pictured it."

"Well, now you've seen it, so let's go back."

"Have you ever climbed up on that rock?" she asks, pointing at the boulder that Alec and I often sit on when we meet here.

"Yes, but not when it's about to rain."

She plays the beam of her flashlight over the boulder and steps closer, running a hand over its surface.

"Please, Eve. Let's go back."

I regret having brought her down here. We'll get soaked if it starts to pour. But she shows no sign of turning back.

I watch her tackle the boulder, determined to climb it. When she finally reaches the top, she stands there, facing the water, and flings out her arms like she's offering herself to the moon, or maybe the universe.

"Come up," she calls down. "The view from here is great."

"I've seen it before."

"You are such a party pooper."

I shove my hands deep into the pockets of my jacket and wonder how long I'll have to wait for her to get tired of standing up there and come down.

Apparently awhile. She sits down cross-legged, palms up, as if she's going to meditate. Her hair is eerily white in the moonlight, her eyes closed. Someone stumbling upon us might think she was a ghost. I'm shivering now. The wind blowing from the ocean is chilly.

"I'm not coming down until you climb up here," she warns.

She probably means it too. I might as well climb the boulder if I don't want to stand here shivering in the rain for the next hour.

The boulder is slippery and hard to climb in the dark. When I get to the top, I drop down beside her. "Satisfied?"

"That wasn't so bad, was it?"

"Now can we go?"

"Do you have your phone?"

I touch the pocket of my jacket and feel the familiar hard shape of my phone. "Why?"

"Let's call Alec."

"I told you. He went to Emmett Falls."

"Yes, I know, but maybe he's on his way back by now."

"But reception is lousy between here and there. I don't think his phone will pick up the signal."

"Humor me."

"No."

I'm tired of Eve's bullying. I'm out of sorts from the steady drizzle, and I'm cold.

She rolls her eyes and reaches in a pocket of her windbreaker. I assume she's going to pull out her own phone, but instead she pulls out a small snub-nose gun.

I stare at it in disbelief.

She grins. "You should see the look on your face."

"Why do you have a gun?"

"In case I need it."

She's pointing it at me. Everything around me seems to come into focus in a way it wasn't before. I'm aware how alone we are, my senses suddenly razor sharp. I feel the hard rock beneath me, the chill in the air, the drizzle on my skin, the growing dampness of my clothes. If I scream, who will hear me? Why was I so stupid as to come here with her?

"Now about that phone call to Alec . . ."

"Please, Eve. Let's go back." I try to keep the fear out of my voice and pretend she doesn't have a gun in her hand aimed at me.

"I want you to phone him."

"Why? I told you. He probably can't get a signal."

"I'll give you until the count of three."

"Why are you doing this?"

"One."

I wonder if I could grab the gun from her. But suppose it goes off? Just like that I could die. My dream of one day being a scientist gone. She could roll my body into the ocean, and the tide would carry me away. No one would know what had happened. My parents would be heartbroken. Alec would think I had run away. No one would know the truth.

"Two."

I don't think she would shoot me, but am I going to wait to find out? Would it really hurt to call Alec? He's probably out of range of a signal, but making the effort might be enough to appease her.

"All right. I'll do it." I speed dial his number and listen to his phone ring, hoping he won't pick up. I don't want him caught up in Eve's sick game, whatever it is.

She keeps the gun pointed at me. On the third ring he answers. Of all times for the network to work, why did it have to be now?

"Jenny. What's up?"

"Where are you?"

"Near Whitby."

Whitby isn't far. His voice is like a lifeline, connecting me to a world that is normal and sane.

"Listen, if you see Eve, be careful," he tells me. "She has a gun. I tried to call you earlier to warn you, but I couldn't get a signal."

My eyes flick to Eve. She can hear every word he says.

"I know."

"Is she there with you?"

"Yes."

"Where are you?"

"At the rocks off the shore road."

"Okay. Let me talk to her."

I hold out the phone to Eve. "He wants to talk to you."

She takes it in her left hand while her right keeps the gun pointed at me.

I hear his words faint but distinct. "If you hurt her . . ."

"That depends on you," Eve answers sweetly. "You know where we are. We'll wait for you—at least for a little while. Maybe thirty minutes. That should give you time to get here. But if I see any blue lights or hear any sirens . . . Well, let's just say it would be too bad for Jenny."

"I don't know if I can get there in thirty minutes."

"Try." She turns off the phone.

I'm shivering, although whether from the cold or fear, I don't know. "What are you going to do?"

"You'll see."

I shouldn't have called Alec. Now I've placed him in danger too. Of course, he'll show up. Anyone else would have the sense to stay away, but not Alec. Knowing he's playing right into Eve's hands won't stop him. He'll come because I'm in trouble, and that's exactly what she's counting on. It's why she wanted me to phone him. She knew he wouldn't refuse. She's probably planning to shoot both of us.

I wonder if I could get the gun away from her? It's risky, but what do I have to lose? *Your life*, answers a voice in my head. *It would take only a split second for her to pull the trigger. Are you so eager to die?*

She tosses me my phone and with the gun still pointed at me stands. "Get up."

I scramble to my feet, jamming the phone back in my pocket. It's raining harder now. The rain beads my eyelashes, my jacket is soaked, my hair is wet, and I'm cold.

"What now?" I ask, trying to keep my teeth from chattering.

"We're going higher." She points with her gun to the next boulder, the massive one that juts out into the water, the one Alec warned me not to climb because of the treacherous rocks below.

CHAPTER 29

Alec

It's raining and my wipers swing back and forth in a fruitless effort to give me a clear view of the road ahead. The headlights of a semi rush toward me out of the darkness, and then the behemoth blasts past and I'm alone again with the wet highway rushing toward me in my high beams. I should slow down, but I worry that I won't get to Jenny in time. On the other hand, if I have an accident, that too could keep me from getting to Sutter's Bend in time to stop Eve from whatever she's bent on doing.

I wonder how she and Jenny ended up at the rocks, but it's not important. What's important is that I get there before anything bad happens to Jenny. I need a plan, but I can't come up with one. My brain is racing like a gerbil on its exercise wheel. I keep coming back to the gun. I could call 911, but Eve threatened to hurt Jenny if she hears a siren or sees flashing blue lights, so I can't take that chance. I just hope Jenny doesn't do anything reckless. If I can get there in time, maybe I can talk Eve out of whatever she has planned. It's hard to believe she'd actually shoot Jenny, but I don't want to make the mistake of underestimating her. I have no idea why she's doing this. Is she trying to punish me because I said I wouldn't marry her? She couldn't seriously have thought I would.

I know a shortcut to the shore road. As I get near, I slow down just enough not to lose control of the car as I veer onto it. I've kept one eye on the clock on my dash ever since the phone call. I'm only a little over the thirty minutes Eve allotted me. Surely she won't shoot Jenny before I get there. It's me she wants to hurt, not Jenny. She's only going after Jenny because she knows how I feel about her. Once I get there, I'll try to persuade her to let Jenny go. I'll promise whatever I have to promise.

The backroad that runs along the shore is twisty, and I curse every time I have to slow down for yet another hairpin turn with a steep drop-off if I miss it. When I finally get to where the shore road overlooks the rocky little strip of beach with the boulders, I see Clara's black BMW and slam on the brakes. The car skids to a stop behind the BMW. I fling the door open and charge down the steep incline at a breakneck pace, pelted by the rain, hoping I'm not too late. When I get down to the beach, I look desperately around for Eve and Jenny but see only rocks and boulders.

"Jenny!" I shout into the wind and rain.

In answer I hear only the waves crashing against the rocks. My heart beats frantically. Then faintly Jenny's voice calls, "Here!"

A beam of light flashes on top of the largest boulder. A figure stands there in the rain, silhouetted against the night sky.

"Are you okay?" I shout.

"Yes!" Jenny's voice.

I run to the boulder I've climbed more times than I can count. I know every inch of it by heart, and soon I'm standing on it.

"That's far enough," Eve shouts from the next boulder, the massive one that juts out into the water. She's the figure I saw standing against the night sky. She holds a flashlight in one hand, a gun in the other pointed at the head of someone crouching beside her—Jenny.

"Come any closer and I'll shoot her."

"You haven't hurt her, have you?"

"No, but I will if you make me."

At least there's still time to save Jenny. But where they are is dangerous.

"Look, why don't you both come down from there, and we'll talk about this?" I shout through the rain.

"No, I like it up here."

"It's not safe."

"I tried to tell her," Jenny shouts. Looking wet and bedraggled, she rests one hand on the rock for balance, her other raised in the classic hands-up position I've seen in a million movies.

"There are rocks under the water," I shout to Eve. "If you slip and fall, they can kill you."

"Do you think I care?" she shouts back.

I know I have to think fast. Jenny's life depends on it.

"Look, let Jenny go. She hasn't done anything to you. It's me you're mad at."

"No!"

"If you want to shoot someone, shoot me."

"Maybe I'll do that anyway."

The gun is almost touching Jenny's forehead. I have to do something. It could go off accidentally. But I don't want to force Eve's hand either. I have no idea how far she's willing to go.

"You don't want to do this," I tell her.

"Don't tell me what I want to do. I'm sick of being told what to do. *I* decide what I want to do."

Keep her talking. But don't say the wrong thing or Jenny will die. Be careful what you say.

"Okay. Just tell me so I understand. Why are you doing this?"

"You really don't know?"

"No, I don't. Why don't the two of you come down here, and we'll talk about it?"

"There's nothing to talk about."

I look at Jenny, still crouched with one hand on the rock and one raised. If I don't think of something fast, Eve is going to shoot her.

"What if I said I'll marry you?"

"I wouldn't believe you."

"But I would if you'd let her go. I give you my word."

"Your word," she scoffs. "Who cares about your word?"

I take a step toward her, calculating the leap I'll need to make to reach the larger boulder. I'm not sure I can do it. As if sensing what I'm thinking, she points the gun at me. Before I can jump, Jenny lunges at her. A loud bang shatters the night as the gun goes off. Then Jenny springs across the distance separating us, and I catch her in my arms. Eve drops to her knees and searches frantically in the dark for the gun she just dropped.

"Are you all right?" I ask Jenny.

"Yes." Her hair is plastered to her head from rain, and I can feel her shivering in my arms, but she's alive and that's all that matters.

I take her hand and hold it tight. "Let's go before she finds the gun."

She glances back at Eve uncertainly. "We can't just leave her here."

"Why not?"

"Look at her."

Eve is alone now on the other boulder, down on her hands and knees, crying and talking to herself. She no longer looks like a threat to anyone. She looks broken.

"What about the gun?" I ask Jenny.

"I think it fell down between the rocks."

Maybe so, but if Eve finds it, we'll be easy targets where we are.

"*Please*." Jenny's eyes plead with me.

Part of me wants to leave Eve there, but maybe Jenny's right. Maybe it would be wrong to walk away and leave her.

"Eve, it's over," I shout.

She gives no sign of hearing me, just plays her flashlight beam erratically over the boulder, searching desperately for the gun.

"She tried to kill you," I remind Jenny.

"I know, but we still can't leave her like this."

"Eve, we're going back now," I shout. "Why don't you come with us?"

She shakes her head. "Too late."

At least I think that's what she said. Her words were muffled, half sobbed.

"Too late for what?"

She stands and takes a step backward, glancing over her shoulder at the waves crashing on the rocks below.

"Careful!" I shout. "There are rocks down there. You don't want to slip and fall."

She ignores my warning and inches closer to the edge.

"Eve, don't!" Jenny shouts.

I try to think of something to say to distract Eve. "I never got to tell you—"

She hesitates, her eyes fixed on the turbulent water. "Tell me what?"

What can I say to draw her attention away? "I never got to tell you what Clara said about you."

She stands perfectly still, staring down at the waves slamming against the boulder.

"What did she say?"

My mind races. "She said you're like a daughter to her."

"She said that?" Her voice quavers. Her eyes are riveted on the waves crashing below.

"Yes. She said she was worried about you when she realized you were gone."

"I don't believe you."

"No, it's true."

"I'm just someone she took in like a stray because she felt sorry for me. And she thought I'd be useful. She doesn't care what happens to me. No one does."

"I'm sure that's not true."

"It is. Nobody cares what happens to me. Nobody has ever cared what happens to me."

"That's no reason to kill yourself," Jenny shouts.

Eve looks over her shoulder at us. "What would you know about it? Either of you. You've had people who cared about you your whole lives. Is anyone ever going to notice me? Does anyone even know I'm alive?"

"You can change your life," I tell her. "You don't have to work for Clara. Find something else to do."

"Like what?"

I remember that day we drove to Eugene. She said she wanted to travel to Venice. "You could be a travel agent or get a job with a cruise line or be an airline attendant. Think of the places you could travel."

She looks at the ocean as if considering this. Maybe I've gotten through to her. If I jump to her boulder, can I reach her in time?

"You could take that trip to Venice for Carnival."

She lifts one hand to her forehead, frowning. "No. It's too late."

I release Jenny and take a flying leap to the boulder on which Eve stands. But my hands grasp empty air as I reach out for her. She's already dropped into the churning water below.

CHAPTER 30

Jenny

After the police arrive, Alec and I give statements and answer a barrage of questions. How did we know Eve? Why were we there? What was her state of mind? Why was she threatening us?

Meanwhile, several officers descend to the shoreline and scramble over the rocks below as the rain continues to fall. From the road we can see their flashlights bobbing about in the dark. Eventually they find the gun and retrieve Eve's body before it washes out to sea.

When they are done with us, Alec drives me home while the police impound Clara's car as evidence. We don't say much on the way. We're both exhausted. When we get to my house, it's dark, my dad and Becca not yet back from the Duck.

"Are you sure you'll be all right?" Alec asks after he walks me to the door. "I can stay if you want."

Much as I would like him to stay, I think it would be better if he weren't here when my father gets home. I'm worried what my father will say when I tell him about what happened tonight. I don't want him to blame Alec. None of it was his fault. Besides, I need some time alone to decompress. But when I step inside the dark house, I almost change my mind. It's so quiet. I feel like I'm listening for something—a dripping faucet, a creaking floorboard, any sign of life. I remember the feeling of Eve's gun pressed to my head, the sense of utter helplessness, the terror of knowing I might be about to die. But I refuse to give in to my fear. I won't let Eve win. I walk resolutely from room to room flipping on lights until the whole house is lit up, and then I go back to the living room and turn on the TV loud enough to drown out the silence.

As I shed my jacket, I notice my clothes are still wet. Once I've noticed, I can't wait another minute to rid myself of them. I head for the bathroom, peel off every stitch of clothing, and turn on the shower full blast as hot as I can bear it. I stay in until I use up all the warm water. Afterward, I feel better. I put on dry clothes and towel dry my hair. Finally I have stopped shaking.

Wiping the steam off the bathroom mirror with a corner of my towel, I look at myself. To my surprise I don't look any different. After what I've been through, it seems like I should look different. My hair should have turned white, or my face should be permanently marked by the violent emotions I felt tonight.

"You're okay," I whisper to my reflection, touching my temple with a forefinger where the barrel of the gun pressed. "You're alive."

I feel like I've been given a second chance at life. I can hardly believe I survived, but here I am, breathing, my life before me. I make a vow to myself not to waste a minute of the precious time I've been given and not to let anyone stop me from doing the things I want to do.

I wander to the kitchen and open the door of the refrigerator. Half of a roast chicken sits on a plate covered by plastic wrap. It occurs to me that I haven't eaten anything since lunch at the hospital. I haul out the chicken, then grab lettuce, mayo, tomato—whatever I can find to go with it. I don't remember ever feeling so hungry before. I'm just finishing off the chicken when I hear the click of the front door unlocking and then voices. I'm still sitting there with the remnants of my feast when Becca and my dad appear in the doorway. For a moment no one says anything as they take in the spread on the table.

"Looks like you were hungry," Becca remarks.

"Why are all the lights on?" my father asks.

"It seemed dark."

He looks at me and waits for more. In the silence I can hear the TV in the living room, still blaring.

"Eve's dead."

He glances at Becca. "Who's Eve?"

CHAPTER 31

Alec

When I get home after dropping Jenny off, the house is dark, which is a relief since it means Toby and Mom must already be in bed. I don't really feel like talking to anyone. I just want to drop into bed and sleep—providing I don't have nightmares about Eve falling from the boulder or floating face down like a broken toy batted about by the breakers. I don't need Eve haunting my dreams.

I take my shoes off and carry them upstairs, trying not to make any noise. But as I'm passing my mother's bedroom, I hear sobbing. I stand there a moment listening. I could keep going and pretend I didn't hear, but my feet seem rooted to the spot. I rap lightly and the sobbing stops.

"Are you okay?" I ask, keeping my voice low so I don't wake Toby.

The door flies open. My mother stands before me in her pajamas, her eyes red and puffy from crying. Her eyes go straight to my shoes, which I'm still holding. All right, she caught me sneaking in. I'm too tired to care.

"Is everything okay?" I repeat.

"He broke up with me." The tears well up again. Her lower lip trembles.

"Roger?"

"Of course, Roger. Who else would it be?"

She collapses on the bed and grabs a fresh tissue from the box sitting there. "He sent me a *text*. Can you believe it? He broke up with me in a text! I feel so humiliated."

"He's a jerk. I told you I didn't like him."

"I feel like nobody will ever love me again. My life is over."

I put down my shoes, sit down beside her, and awkwardly put my arms around her. Our roles feel oddly reversed. It's like I'm the parent and she's the teen. I feel sorry for her. Being rejected sucks no matter what age you are.

"Your life isn't over," I tell her. "Of course, you're going to find someone else."

"You really think so?" Her lip is still trembling.

"I know so."

"When did you get so grown up?"

"Last year I think."

She gives a choked laugh and pushes me away, frowning. "You're wet."

"It was raining."

"What did you do, stand out in it to see how wet you could get?"

"Something like that."

She narrows her eyes suspiciously, her maternal instincts kicking in. "What are you not telling me?"

I don't feel like lying. The truth is going to come out soon enough. In fact, it'll probably be on the front page of tomorrow's newspaper. The crowd at her watercooler will go wild.

"Eve's dead."

Her eyes widen. "Eve Nielsen? How do you know?"

"Because I was there."

She looks shocked. "What? When did this happen?"

"Earlier this evening. North of town. Off the shore road."

"What happened?"

"She fell off a boulder into the water. It was raining. There were rocks down below."

My mother springs up. "Wait a minute. She called here earlier. Jenny was here."

"Jenny was there too."

"They must have gone there after she was here. Jenny was going to meet her, although I told her she shouldn't."

"Eve had a gun."

"*What?*"

"She was going to shoot Jenny. I tried to talk her down."

The whole awful scene rears up in front of me again. I feel as if I'm going to be sick.

"Is Jenny all right?"

"Yes, but Eve—" I see again Eve stepping off the boulder as casually as one would step into the street.

"Oh, honey." She puts her arms around me. Now it's her turn to comfort me. The tears come then. I can't stop them. I don't know if I'm crying for Eve or for me.

I struggle to explain. "You see, I don't think it was an accident. I think she killed herself. I just don't understand why."

"Oh, baby, nobody understands things like that."

"I tried. I really did. I thought I could talk her out of it. But I didn't know how to do it."

"Of course, you didn't. Who would?"

I feel grateful she doesn't blame me, but how do I stop blaming myself? I feel like Eve's death is a regret I'm going to carry with me for the rest of my life.

CHAPTER 32

Jenny

There are already a number of friends and relatives of the family at the funeral home when Alec and I arrive. Eve's stepsister Danielle, a dark-haired girl with a quick smile who looks nothing at all like Eve, greets us soon after we walk in the door. After introducing herself, she thanks us for coming.

"I'm sorry about Eve," she says, as if she had any responsibility for Eve's actions. "She had a dark side to her. Everyone knew that. She always scared me a little when we were growing up. It was a relief when she left home."

It seems an odd thing to say at a sister's funeral. I remember what Eve said about a stepsister not being the same as a real sister. Apparently the feeling was mutual.

"So you weren't close?"

"No. She didn't like it when my dad married her mom. She used to pull my hair and sometimes things of mine would disappear. Clothes. A ring once. A butterfly pin that belonged to my mother. I think she was jealous."

"What about the car accident?" Alec asks.

"What car accident?"

"The one on an icy bridge."

Danielle rolls her eyes. "Eve was always making things up. Mom thought working for Clara might help her. She arranged the job. I'm not sure it made any difference. We just saw less of her."

"Did Eve have many friends?" I look about the room and notice almost everyone is older than us. I'm surprised there aren't more young people.

"A couple of girlfriends. Some boyfriends." She lowers her voice. "She was pregnant, you know."

Alec stiffens. "No, that's not possible."

She gives him a curious sidelong look. "It was in the police report."

I hold Alec's hand tighter. "Do you know who the father was?"

She shakes her head. "Not really, but I did see her post about how she was going to get married." Another sidelong look at Alec. No doubt she knows he was the subject of that post.

"She made that up, you know," I tell Danielle.

"Oh, yes. Clara explained it all to us. Like I said, Eve often made up things. Maybe to get attention. Who knows?"

The door to the funeral home swings open again, and a tall young man with a ponytail steps into the room.

"Oh, there's Carl," Danielle says. "Excuse me. I have to talk to him."

At that moment I notice Mrs. Duncan pushing Clara in her wheelchair in our direction.

"It was good of you to come," Clara says, reaching out her hand when they are close. "So glad to see you both again, but sorry it's under such sad circumstances."

"How are you holding up?" I ask.

"Oh, tolerably. I blame myself. I feel I should have done more for Eve. I thought her therapist would help her find her way. She seemed to be doing so well."

"I didn't know she was seeing a therapist. She never mentioned it." I glance at Alec.

"No, I didn't know."

"Eve had her troubles," Clara says. "Such a shame that she died so young." She pats my hand. "What about you, Jenny? Is your plan to attend college in the fall still on hold?"

"Yes. We still don't know what's going to happen with my mom."

"That's your gardener, isn't it?" Alec says, looking at the young man with the ponytail, his head bent to listen to Danielle, who is talking animatedly to him.

"Carl?" Clara asks.

"Yes, that's him," Mrs. Duncan answers for her.

"Were he and Eve close?" I ask.

"They were friends," Clara says. "She recommended him. They met at that festival in Nevada."

"Burning Man," Alec mutters.

"That's right. Burning Man. He's a wonderful gardener but very shy. Doesn't say much."

I glance at the young man with the ponytail again, wondering just how close a friend of Eve's he might have been.

"Have you met Eve's mother?" Mrs. Duncan asks as a woman in an immaculate white suit and high heels approaches us. She has Eve's white-blonde hair and pale blue eyes. Around her neck she wears a string of pearls.

"Clara, how well you're looking."

"This is Alec and Jenny," Clara says, introducing us.

A shock of recognition flits across the woman's face as she realizes who we are. Then she smiles, all poise and unruffled self-assurance again.

"I'm sorry if my daughter caused you any distress."

It seems an odd thing to say. And of course, like Danielle, she's not responsible for what Eve did.

As if realizing something more may be called for, she confides, "Eve wasn't an easy child to raise. She threw temper tantrums when she was little."

This revelation also seems odd and hardly explains what happened at the rocks.

"Many children have temper tantrums," I suggest, resisting the urge to add that they don't usually grow up to be dangerous.

"I suppose so. But Eve was always a little different. I thought Danielle would be a good companion for her. You know—a sister. What girl doesn't want a sister? But from the beginning she took a dislike to Danielle."

"You did the best you could," Clara assures her. "You tried to be a good mother."

"I did," says Eve's mother, fingering her pearls.

"Is Eve's father here?" Alec asks, looking about.

"Not likely. He hasn't been in her life for years. Not since we divorced."

"Her stepfather then?"

"No, he's abroad just now—on business."

Mrs. Duncan clears her throat. "Eve seemed a bit of a lost soul. I felt a little sorry for her. She didn't seem to have many friends."

"Yes, she struck me as lonely," I add.

Mrs. Nielsen stands straighter. "Well, if she was, it was her own fault. She pushed everyone away." Maybe she spoke more sharply than she intended. Or maybe she realizes it sounds unkind to criticize the dead. She looks around as if seeking a way out of a conversation that has turned awkward. Seeing someone she knows, she excuses herself.

"Well, that was a bit cold, wasn't it?" Mrs. Duncan says in a low voice.

Clara looks troubled. "I'm sure she's more upset than she lets on. It isn't easy to lose a child."

No doubt she's thinking of the loss of her own daughter so many years ago. I reach out and touch her hand.

"We don't choose our families," Alec whispers in my ear. "You think Eve may have been right when she said she wasn't loved? There didn't seem like a lot of love lost there."

Before I can answer, the double doors to the next room swing wide and it's time to file into the chapel for the service.

CHAPTER 33

Alec

Sutter's Bend doesn't get many drownings, accidental or otherwise. For a while Jenny and I are local celebrities. People seem to forget Eve's claim that I got her pregnant and see us as the would-be victims of a mentally deranged young woman. But I think it's more complicated than that, although I doubt I can explain it to anyone, including myself.

One good result, though, is I got my job back at the Bookery. Mrs. Kilmer isn't thrilled about it, but Liv says she's glad she no longer has to worry about standing in for Mrs. Kilmer during the Children's Hour if she's ever out sick.

My life is slowly returning to normal when one afternoon I get off work early and arrive home to find a grey Nissan with rental plates parked in our drive. I eye it warily, wondering who it belongs to. Hopefully not yet another reporter with questions about Eve's death. My uneasiness increases when I discover our front door unlocked. Stepping inside, I hear the TV going and recognize one of Toby's favorite shows, but there's no sign of Toby. I wonder if he could have answered the door and let someone in he shouldn't have? He has strict instructions not to let anyone in he doesn't know when Mom's not home. If he disobeyed, he's going to be in trouble.

I hear voices upstairs, so I quietly climb the stairs to see who's there. Halfway up, I recognize Toby's voice. A few steps more, and I recognize my dad's. He's back! I can't believe it. After all this time, and after putting Mom through so much grief. I feel relieved and annoyed with him at the same time. I wonder if he knows about Roger-Dodger. If he doesn't, I won't be the one to tell him. Let Mom explain about Roger.

They're in my parents' bedroom. From the doorway I see an open suitcase and several boxes on the bed. My dad is folding clothes into them. The truth hits me like a two-by-four. This isn't a change of heart. He's come back for the rest of his clothes and other belongings. I'll bet he deliberately timed his visit for when Mom would be at work, sneaked in to grab his things, and plans to be gone before she comes home.

"What are you doing?" I ask.

He looks up. "Alec. When did you get home?"

"Just now."

"Perfect timing. I get to say goodbye to both my boys." He grins at Toby, who's sitting cross-legged on the bed between the boxes and the suitcase.

"I don't want you to say goodbye," Toby protests. "Why can't you stay?"

"I already explained, buddy. Your mom and I decided it's better this way. Better for you and Alec. Better for everybody."

Better for *him*, he means.

"Does Mom know you're here?" I ask.

"I'll leave her a note."

I watch him toss a couple of sweaters into the suitcase. He's wearing a T-shirt I've never seen before with a logo for the Toronto Raptors. "You're going back to Canada?"

"Yeah."

"Will we ever see you again?"

"Sure." Another glance at Toby.

"When?"

"I don't know. You can write me. Or text me. Or phone. We'll stay in touch."

He avoids looking me in the eye. I think of all the times I've texted or tried to phone him. I know how that goes. We're part of his past and he's ready to move on.

"Anyway, you're practically out of here yourself."

He thinks that makes it okay? I feel a surge of anger. "I'm not going to study premed," I tell him. Might as well be sure he understands that.

"Yeah, you told me. So what are you going to study? Or don't you know?"

I see the smirk. He thinks he knows me but he doesn't. A few weeks ago I wouldn't have had an answer for him. Now I do.

"Psychology."

"A psych major? Really? You want to be a shrink and get paid to listen to other people's problems?" He shakes his head in disbelief.

"I want to understand people better and help them."

He gives me a skeptical look. "Does this have something to do with that girl who died?"

"Maybe."

"I think you're making a mistake."

Of course, he does. In his mind any major I choose that doesn't lead to a medical degree is a mistake. If he thinks a medical degree is so great, why didn't he get one?

"Does that mean you won't pay my tuition?"

He rubs the back of his neck. "I don't have much choice about that. It's part of my agreement with your mother."

I watch him dump the contents of a drawer into the suitcase. He seems to be packing faster. Maybe he's eager to leave now that I'm here. I'm not the pushover Toby is. He didn't count on me being home. I suppose I should turn and walk away but I can't. He's still my dad, and it could be the last time I'll see him. Once he has a new family, who knows if he'll want to have anything to do with Toby and me again.

"What about the Chen girl?" he asks as he looks around the room for anything he missed or maybe for a last look at what he's leaving behind.

"What about her?"

"You can do better, Alec. Don't do something impulsive you'll regret for the rest of your life. You've got your whole life ahead of you. I don't want you to make the mistakes I made."

"You mean marrying Mom? You mean me and Toby?"

He glances at Toby. "Of course not. When you're older, you'll understand."

"Will I?"

He sighs. "Look, this is hard enough. You don't have to make it even harder."

"You think this isn't hard on us?"

"I'm sorry about that."

Who knows, maybe he is. Maybe his choice will look different when I'm older. Maybe everything will. Except Jenny. I'm pretty sure my feelings for her aren't going to change.

CHAPTER 34

Jenny

I'm fixing breakfast for Mom when the doorbell rings.

"Can you get it?" Becca shouts from our bedroom, where she's supposedly meditating. She just took up meditating recently. Knowing how bored she gets when she's not doing anything, I'll bet she's actually texting a friend.

I'm boiling a couple of eggs—nothing that can't wait—so I leave the eggs, dash through the living room, and fling open the front door.

A UPS delivery man stands there with a large envelope addressed to me, signature required. I sign for it, wondering what it could be. Then I carry it back to the kitchen and rip it open while the eggs continue to boil. It takes a minute or two for me to process what I'm looking at. Letterhead stationery from MIT. It looks official. They're offering me a tuition-free scholarship. However, to receive the scholarship I must first apply for admission by completing and returning the enclosed application packet. I shuffle through the packet, then read the letter again. It's got to be a mistake. Colleges don't offer scholarships to students who haven't applied, as far as I know.

They must have meant to send it to some other prospective student. A different Jenny Chen. And even if by some weird twist of fate it's meant for me, I can't accept it. Not with my mom's health so uncertain. My family needs me here. *She* needs me here.

"What is it?" My mom stands in the doorway looking like a strong wind might blow her away. Once more the sight of her makes me feel as if someone is squeezing my heart. Of course I can't leave her.

I push the packet aside on the counter, hoping she won't notice, and turn my attention back to the eggs. "Almost ready."

"You know, I could do that," she says, stepping closer.

"Why should you? I've already done it."

"Who was at the door?"

"Nothing important."

"Did something come for you?"

I glance guiltily at the envelope. "It's nothing. Junk mail."

"Oh? May I see it?"

I can't very well refuse. "It's a mistake, I think. MIT. I didn't even apply there."

She takes the papers and spreads them out on the counter. "It looks like they're offering you a tuition-paid scholarship."

"Yes, but it has to be a mistake."

"I don't think it's a mistake, Jenny."

"But I can't accept it."

"Why not?"

"Because I'm going to wait a year or two. That's what we decided. Now is not a good time."

"Because of me?"

"Well, yes, but . . ."

"You can't just postpone your life because of me. I don't want you to."

Why doesn't she think it strange MIT would offer me a scholarship out of the blue? She must understand this isn't how it works. Suddenly I'm suspicious.

"You don't seem very surprised. Do you know something about this?"

She smiles. "Clara called a couple of days ago."

"Clara?"

"She arranged this. She said she wanted to do something for you. She said MIT has one of the best programs for biochemistry."

"Why didn't she tell me?"

"She wanted it to be a surprise."

"But I can't accept this."

"Of course you can."

"But MIT? It's so far away. If I were at University of Oregon, at least I could come home."

"You can come home from anywhere."

Tears blur my eyes. I remember the eggs I'm boiling and grab a potholder. I've probably overcooked them.

CHAPTER 35

Alec

Jenny snuggles against me, and it feels so right. We are sitting on our rock looking out over the ocean at the deepening orange of the sunset. Her hair blows against my face. Seagulls swoop and dive over the water while waves crash against the rocks.

For a while after Eve's death we were reluctant to come back to this strip of rocky shoreline, but in the end we agreed we weren't going to let Eve take it away from us. She had already taken away too much.

"Are you thinking about her?" Jenny asks.

"I guess so. Hard not to."

"I think about her a lot. Every day in fact."

"So do I."

"Do you suppose a time will come when we don't think about her so much?"

"I hope so."

"I should never have let her persuade me to come here that night."

"You couldn't have known what she would do."

"I felt sorry for her. I think it kept me from seeing she might be dangerous. She didn't seem dangerous—not until that last night."

"I felt uncomfortable with her from the start. I think deep down I knew something was off about her."

"You say that now, but she seemed normal enough to me when I first met her."

"I should never have let her go with me to Eugene and I should never have let her stay that night at the motel."

"I don't think she brought me here that night because of you. I think it was because of me. She didn't want to kill you. She wanted to kill me."

"Maybe so, but she wanted me to *watch*."

"But it was me she hated, not you," Jenny insists. "She saw me as having things she wanted. She told me that."

"She wanted to break us up, regardless of why. We'll probably never know why."

"You have to admit, it was a rather extreme way to do it."

I kiss her forehead. Summer is almost over. Tomorrow she leaves for the East Coast, and next week I leave for Eugene. I'll miss coming here with her. Sutter's Bend won't seem the same without her.

"Maybe you'll forget me when you're off at MIT," I tell her. "You'll meet some brainy guy who understands physics and can recite the periodic table backward."

"Maybe you'll meet someone at University of Oregon and forget about me."

"I doubt it."

"I wish we could be together."

"I do too, but this is your chance to do what you've always dreamed of. I want you to have that chance."

She grimaces. "They say long distance romances are hard."

"They're probably right."

"You won't forget me?"

"I could never forget you. Besides, we'll text. We'll talk. I'll send you copies of all the good horror novels I run across."

She jabs me playfully in the ribs with her elbow. "Christmas then?"

"Count on it."

She tilts her head up and our lips meet. I don't really want to think about the future. I have to trust that we'll find our way back to each other. For now, this moment is what matters, being here with Jenny, holding her in my arms as the waves crash and the gulls wheel overhead.

ABOUT THE AUTHOR

DEANNA MADDEN is the author of *Helena Landless, Gaslight and Fog, The World Beyond: A Novel of Ancient Greece*, and other novels. Originally from Indiana, she has taught literature and creative writing at colleges in Miami, Florida; upstate New York; and Hawaii. She currently lives in Honolulu, where she enjoys the trade winds and sunshine when she takes a break from writing.